Watch for More Novels by Lindsay Luterman

from Indigo Sea Press

indigoseapress.com

Mercy's Sunset

By

Lindsay Luterman

Perseverance Books
Published by Indigo Sea Press
Winston-Salem

Perseverance Books
Indigo Sea Press
302 Ricks Drive
Winston-Salem, NC 27103

First Perseverance Books edition published
January, 2016
Perseverance Books, Moon Sailor and all production design are
trademarks of Indigo Sea Press, used under license.

For information regarding bulk purchases of this book, digital
purchase and special discounts, please contact the publisher at
indigoseapress.com

Cover design by Stacy Castanedo

Manufactured in the United States of America
ISBN 978-1-63066-343-8

In loving memory of

Marlene Katz

Prologue
The Awakening

I jolted upwards, my eyes shooting straight open as I screamed, "Mercy!"

I was met with silence that seemed to wrap around me. It was bright, and calm, and strikingly eerie, as if all the sound had been sucked up into a black hole and it took everything else with it… except me.

Where was I?

I wracked my brain for an answer. When I couldn't find one, I tried to fill in the hole in my memory that could possibly answer how I got here. When I came back short of that, I became so frustrated, knowing I was doing something very important, completing a mission that couldn't be ignored, and I was torn away from it. Now I had to get back because if I don't complete this mission…

Wait a second. Why couldn't I finish that sentence?

If I didn't complete this mission…

Nothing. I knew absolutely nothing and it was so aggravating and frightening that I began to panic. I should know the answer. For the first time, I actually took a look at my surroundings. But just like my thoughts, all I saw was… nothing. It was not just the kind of 'no furniture' nothing. No, it was the kind of nothing that meant that the world was blank. Just a never-ending whiteness.

The panic turned to downright fear. Where was I? Where was everybody? Where was *anything*?

I jumped to my feet and found that there was nothing holding me down. I felt so light, like air. I gasped loudly and felt the first sting of tears. "Help!" I cried. "Please! Somebody! Where am I?"

My eyes shot back and forth and I spun around and

around but found nothing to ease my worry. I began to shake, my stomach twisting and my knees feeling weak, but there was something missing. I tried to calm my breathing, trying to slow my heartbeat. It was all second nature. And then it hit me.

My heartbeat!

My hands pressed tightly over my chest, barely finding any flesh, much less a heartbeat. I was almost see-though, so translucent that I could practically press my hands right through my chest. I was nearly nothing.

I was so wrapped up in my confusion that I lost my footing when a slight breeze washed straight through me. My scream was mixed with a sob as I landed flat on my face, only to be blinded with more whiteness.

But this time, I heard something else. Soft, even footsteps walking toward me. They sounded so sure, so perfect and fluent. They weren't human. A swift chill ran up my spine, and I didn't move until the footsteps stopped right next to my face.

I slowly picked my head up and saw a hand right in front of it. I didn't trust it, but I didn't trust anything else either. My shaking hand gradually slid forwards and I grasped onto the pale, slender, perfect hand that was held out to me. It pulled me upwards and every inch that I was pulled revealed the rest of the body that the hand belonged to. Its feet were masked by a long silk gown, but I could see the outline of its body; legs, hips, chest, shoulders, arms, neck, and –finally— face.

She was flawless: perfect skin, pale grey eyes, straight nose, full red lips, and thick blond hair that flowed all the way down her back. She blinked once, flashing long eyelashes and then giggled softly with a voice so pure that it sounded surreal. "Tell me," she said, gently bringing my hand down to my side and then releasing it. "Why were you yelling, 'Mercy'?"

My breath caught in my throat as I stared at her and I was barely able to form the words. "I don't... I can't..." I stammered through sentences unintelligibly and then gave up trying, my voice failing me.

"Well then, can you tell me your name?" she asked, lowering her face a bit and staring up through her eyelashes. "I'm not quite sure what to call you."

I nodded slowly and my lips quivered as I tried to get the answer out. "M-my name is..." I lost my train of thought.

The truth was that I didn't know. How did I not know my own name? I opened my mouth again, but this time only a cry escaped.

"Don't know, huh?" the lady asked.

I shook my head.

She sighed and smiled softly. "Well then make something up," she said. "I can call you whatever you'd like. I just need something to address you by."

I swallowed thickly and shook my head, feeling it ache from so much thinking. I put my hand back over my heart and pressed tightly, trying to find a heartbeat but coming up empty again.

"Searching for a heartbeat?" she whispered. I nodded. "Well you won't find one. As for your name, we might just have to call you Jane Doe like they do in hospitals when an unidentified patient is taken in. That is, unless you have anything better in mind."

"N-no," I stuttered hoarsely, choking on tears. "Jane Doe is fine."

The lady nodded her head. "Aren't you going to ask my name?" she asked in a cool, clear voice. When I didn't answer, she answered for me. "My name is Thyme."

"Time?" I asked. "Like the clock?"

"No, like the herb."

"Okay," I said softly and scratched nervously at my arm.

"My, my. You are a quiet one. Most people have tons of questions to ask. Are you telling me that you have no questions?"

I just stared at her with wide eyes and my mouth opened and closed a few times, but no words came out.

"Or are you just afraid?" Thyme questioned with a bit more understanding to her tone. "Ah, I see. Well I can inform you that there is no need to fear, Jane Doe. You are safe here. The only thing you have to do is decide."

I squinted in confusion and forced myself to speak. "Decide what?" I croaked.

"She speaks!" Thyme cheered. "What a relief. This makes it so much easier."

"Makes what so much easier? And what do I have to decide?" I gasped out, watching as Thyme tapped the tips of her fingers against each other. "Answer me!" I cried.

Thyme stepped back a little, her eyes wide with surprise. It soon faded and a miniscule smile appeared. "Do you remember anything?" she asked instead. "Close your eyes and see what comes to mind."

"But I—"

"Just try it," she coaxed. "Just close your eyes and tell me what you see."

As much as she scared me— as much as I hated to trust her— I did it anyway for reasons that I was not very sure of. I think it was more for me than it was for her. I needed to remember something, anything. So I allowed my eyes to fall shut and was swarmed with a flood of images and sounds.

Red hair flew in the breeze as the wind blew loudly. Screams echoed through the night with images of darkness and scrawny fingers drenched in blood. Loud booms echoed as fists come in contact with the wall. A young girl who ran through a field of flowers faded into a woman who rushed alongside a road screaming, "Mercy!" which faded

4

into a bright pink, orange, and blue, cloud-filled sky.

My eyes snapped open and a loud, tear-filled gasp echoed through the never-ending world of nothingness. I pressed my hands against my chest tighter, practically begging for a heartbeat and bent over as sobs wracked through me.

"I take it that you remembered something," a voice said from behind me and I spun around in shock, having forgotten all about Thyme.

"Yes. I saw and heard things." I took a deep breath and continued on in a raspy voice. "But I have no idea what they mean!"

Thyme just nodded and pursed her lips. "That's to be expected," she said. "You see Jane Doe, you do not remember because your mind needs a rest so that when the memories do come, you won't remember some more than others and pick those just because they are clearer."

"Pick them for *what*?" I shrieked, losing my patience quickly as my chest heaved with gasps.

"You'll see," Thyme sighed. "It's normal to be confused after death—"

"Dead?" I choked out. "I'm—"

"Dead? Yes, you are. I thought you figured it out by now," Thyme said.

"So what am I supposed to do?" I begged, feeling my limbs beginning to shake with fear.

Thyme smiled warmly and continued. "I can't tell you that," Thyme said. "You must decide. Which is exactly why we are doing this."

"Doing what?" I demanded. "And what do I have to decide?"

Thyme held out her hand and grabbed my translucent fingers, lifting my hand until it was held up against the blinding whiteness that surrounded us. I could see the light shining through it. My hand began to fill with color until it took on a solid texture with a pale skin tone. "Let's start from the beginning, Jane Doe."

Part One
Olivia

The white light turned into the pale pink paint of the small walls that surrounded me. But these walls had an end to them. There was a small crib to the right of the room, next to a big window that took up half of one of the walls. There was a closet to the left and a cushiony pink rocking chair in the corner. A strip of wallpaper ran across the middle of the walls with tiny stencils of the same ballerina; each one showing how she changed position, spinning and spinning across the wall. I took in the achingly familiar room and felt the déjà vu begin to settle in. "Where are we?" I whispered.

"Welcome back to your first life," Thyme said from behind me, a knowing smile on her face. She stepped forward, standing next to me. I watched a car rush by outside through the window behind the crib. It was a very old car, one of the first models. "But I don't understand—"

"Stop talking or you'll miss the show," Thyme hissed, and before I could question what she was talking about, the door opened and an older woman with pasty skin and graying hair pulled up into a tight bun stepped into the room.

An overwhelming sense of recognition rushed through me and I felt tears come to my eyes all over again as a pained feeling clutches at my un-beating heart. "Anita?" I gasped, walking forwards towards the woman who didn't hear a word I said. The name just hit me. "Anita!"

"She can't hear you," Thyme informed me. "It's not even worth trying."

I wiped at my face, watching as Anita delicately lay a sleeping baby down into the crib, smiling with pride as if it were her own child. There was something my mind was hiding from me; some story that I had yet to see. Anita, alive and well right in front of me, had to be the most assuring thing that I had seen since I awoke in this hell-hole.

"Anita!" a strong woman's voice called as footsteps clicked down the hallway. She had a British accent. "Anita! Is the baby asleep yet?"

The young child in the crib began to stir and whimper as a tall woman with dyed, damaged, black hair that was scraped tightly into a ponytail, entered the room. She was wearing so much makeup that she looked fake. She had on a long dress.

The second I saw her, I had a feeling in my gut. I loved her but I hated her all at once. She stomped into the room. "Anita, I just asked you if the baby was asleep yet," she snapped.

The baby opened her big green eyes and let out a loud wail. "She was," Anita said dryly under her breath, carrying the same accent as the other woman.

The tall woman huffed out a deep, angry breath and reached into the crib, awkwardly yanking the baby into her arms and beginning to rock her back and forth. "Olivia," she cooed, sounding very rushed and annoyed. "Darling. It's time to go to sleep."

Anita cleared her throat. "With all due respect Mrs. Harper, talking to her will not put her to sleep. It will just keep her up. She's half asleep to begin with. Just lay her back in her crib."

Mrs. Harper turned to her quickly, scowling. "Do me a favor Anita; don't tell me how to raise my own child." She shoved Olivia back into Anita's arms and the small baby began to cry even louder. "Put her to sleep. I'm late for the council meeting."

Anita forced a polite smile, creating lines around her mouth. "Of course," she said.

Mrs. Harper nodded at her and turned to leave the room. Anita's smile dropped almost instantly. The lines around her mouth faded away. Thyme stepped up next to me and whistled loudly, letting the sound fade. "I would not want her to be my mother," she said.

I shook my head slowly, staring at the door where Mrs. Harper just left. "I think she *is* my mother," I whispered.

Anita stepped over to the pink rocking chair and settled down into the cushions, still holding the crying baby in her arms. She began to rock Olivia back and forth, singing a song to her that was achingly familiar.

"Sweet little girl, please don't cry.
It's time to rest now. Close your eyes.
Your dreams will hold you in their arm,
Keep you happy and safe from harm."

Tears filled my eyes and cascaded down my cheeks silently as the baby grew quiet. "I recognize that song! Why do I know that song?" I gasped out.

Thyme rolled her eyes. "Because you've heard it before, haven't you?"

Thyme walked towards Anita, who was gazing at the now-sleeping Olivia. I felt frustration bubbling inside of me. There were so many unanswered questions, so many things confusing me. Anita began to sing the song again.

"Sweet little girl, I'm right here.
I will not let you go my dear…"

I was suddenly overwhelmed with the eerie tune of the song that I knew I'd heard before, but I didn't know from where. All I knew is that I lived this already. Somehow…

"Stop!" I shouted, catching Thyme's attention.

Anita froze in the rocking chair and the baby in her arms fell completely still. The sounds of movement outside became silent. The whole world was unmoving. "Thyme," I whispered, suddenly afraid. "What did I do?"

"You paused it," she told me. "This is like a movie to

9

you. You control it. You have the remote. Now can you press play? Or better yet, say fast forward. I think we've seen enough of this."

I stepped around her, kneeling down to run my fingers over the baby's head softly, but they went right through. Her skin looked delicate, her hair a light red, so light that I almost didn't see it against her skin. My current skin tone was the same as hers. "I'm Olivia, aren't I?"

"Why don't you press play?" Thyme said, bending down beside me.

I let out a huge breath and muttered, "Play."

Anita began to rock in the chair again, slowing until she came to a stop. She stood up and walked over to the crib, placing Olivia into it. "Sleep well angel," she whispered.

I closed my eyes and felt my head begin to spin.

The Opera

When I opened my eyes, I was no longer in the little pink room and my head was spinning. I was now standing in the back of a theater. It was tightly packed with people who sat in red, fabric seats. On the stage, a woman sang so loudly that it hurt my ears. "Where are we?" I yelled to Thyme who was standing next to me.

"The opera," she responded.

I spotted a young girl who was tugging on her mother's sleeve, trying to get her attention. Her mother was clearly annoyed. I recognized her almost immediately. "Mrs. Harper," I said, mostly to myself, but Thyme overheard. "Is that Olivia?" I asked, nodding toward the young girl with the thick, long red hair and the big green eyes. She must have been four or five years old. Her hair was pulled back into a braid and she wore a red, velvet dress.

"They grow up so fast," Thyme joked and I ignored her, walking towards Olivia and her mother.

Their seats were on a higher level, which was reserved for them. I wanted to get up there, and the second I thought it, I appeared in front of them. They couldn't see me of course. A man, who I assumed must be Mr. Harper, sat with them. I nearly smiled when I saw him. He had thick grey hair and tired-looking green eyes. He was slightly overweight. "Father?" I whispered.

Mrs. Harper wore a black, long-sleeved dress that reached just to her knees and black dress shoes. Her hair was pulled into a tight bun. Mr. Harper was in a suit, his hair brushed back. I could smell his strong cologne. The scent was so familiar.

Olivia continued to pull at her mother's sleeve. "Mama, I'm bored," she whined.

I didn't blame her. The opera was sung in a different language and I didn't recognize a word of it. It sounded like

11

it might be Italian. "Mama," Olivia whimpered.

"Olivia, stop that!" Mrs. Harper warned in a hushed tone.

"But I'm hungry," Olivia said, tugging harder at the sleeve. "Mama!"

"Olivia!" Mrs. Harper hissed, yanking her sleeve away and leaning towards the young girl until their faces were inches apart. "This is your last warning. You better knock it off with the whining and complaining or you will be in a lot of trouble! Do you understand me?"

Olivia whimpered quietly and turned away so fast that she bumped heads with Mrs. Harper. "Ouch!" Mrs. Harper gasped quietly. "That's it!"

She grasped Olivia's hand and began to pull her out of her seat. "No! Stop!" Olivia begged. "It was an accident. I'll stop! I promise!"

Mr. Harper quickly stood up and blocked the doorway that they were headed towards. "Stop it and sit down Julia! This is ridiculous. This is the opera. Of course she won't understand it."

A few people shushed them. Tears were silently running down Olivia's face. I kneeled down beside her, trying to drown out the loud music in the background. "Don't you love the opera? So dramatic!" a voice said from beside me, and I jumped back up to my feet.

Thyme leaned against the balcony, watching everything. "Could you stop appearing like that?" I demanded, throwing my hand over my still heart.

She shrugged. "You really should be used to it by now."

Olivia sunk down into the chair between her parents, clinging to her father and leaning as far away from her mother as possible. Mrs. Harper glared malevolently. As I looked around, I felt disgust. "I remember this theater," I whispered. "I hated it."

Thyme giggled as she watched the woman on stage singing. "Why am I watching this?" I asked. "What's so important about this moment?"

Thyme nodded towards Mr. Harper who looked just about as bored as Olivia. Olivia had tears in her eyes while Julia scowled at the stage. "Looks like a pretty sad family," I observed.

Olivia cuddled up closer to Mr. Harper, resting her head against his black jacket and closing her eyes. Mrs. Harper leaned over. "Olivia it is rude to sleep in here. Olivia—"

"Julia please," Mr. Harper muttered. "Just leave her alone."

Julia looked astonished. She pressed her hand flat against her chest dramatically. "Me? Henry, did you not see her behavior before?"

Henry ran his fingers through his hair and took a deep breath. "Stop acting like a child," he said to her.

Olivia pretended that she was already asleep, keeping her eyes sealed shut. "I want to leave," Julia said. "You've ruined the opera for me!"

"Fine," Henry hissed and lifted Olivia up from her seat.

Olivia squeezed her eyes shut tighter, trying to keep up the act. Julia collected her fur coat from the chair and pulled it on before exiting through the door. Mr. Harper followed. I walked after them, blinking as the bright lights from the hallway blinded me. The carpets were red and the walls were gold. There was a stand where somebody was selling drinks and snacks. The Harpers stormed past all of this, completely ruining the surrounding calm. The singing grew silent as the door shut behind us and my ears began to ring. The anger from the family rolled off of them in waves and began to make me uncomfortable. I closed my eyes for a moment, willing for this to move forward. I couldn't watch this anymore. When I opened my eyes, I was back in the small pink room. It was dark now; the only light came from a small candle from the corner of the room. The crib had been replaced with a bed. Henry entered the room and placed Olivia down onto the bed. It was only later that night and she was still wearing the velvet red dress.

Anita knocked quietly on the door and then entered the room. She wore a robe over her night gown. Her grey hair was long and it hung down to her waist now that it was no longer in a bun. "Anita," Henry grinned, though his eyes were exhausted. "I'm glad you're here. Could you please help Olivia into her pajamas?"

"Of course," she said, nodding and walking over to the girl in the bed.

Henry kissed Olivia on the head. "I think I better be prepared to sleep on the settee," he joked quietly.

Anita frowned. "That bad, huh?"

He shrugged. "Let's just say that my wife is not happy with me," he told her, clearly trusting her more than Julia did.

Anita walked over to the small closet and opened it up, collecting a nightgown. "I'm sure Mrs. Harper will get over it. She loves you."

Henry shrugged, running his fingers through his hair once again. "I sure hope so," he said. "Goodnight Anita."

"Good night Mr. Harper," Anita responded.

Henry left the room and shut the door quietly behind him. The second he was gone, Olivia peeked an eye open. Anita placed her hands on her hips. "You've been awake this entire time, listening to our conversation?" she said disapprovingly.

Olivia looked away guiltily. "I'm sorry," she whispered. "I was just pretending to be asleep so my mother wouldn't be angry. She got so mad at me before." Olivia sat up and slammed her tiny fists against the bed repeatedly. "I hate her! I hate her! I hate her!"

Anita gasped and sat down on the bed, grasping the

young girl's hands in her own to still them. "You don't hate her," she said, sounding worried. "She's your mother."

"So?" Olivia began biting her nails.

Anita grasped Olivia's wrists, pulling them away from her face. "So, just because she may yell doesn't mean she doesn't love you and that you shouldn't love her back."

Olivia shrugged, her shoulders lifting up and down in a swift movement. "Well I can't love her when I hate her."

Anita sighed deeply and reached for the small, sky-blue nightgown. "Put this on," she instructed.

Olivia reached her short arms behind her body and attempted to unzip the dress, but her hands didn't quite reach. Anita unzipped it for her in one swift movement. Olivia pulled the dress off of her body and tossed it to the floor, reaching to pull the nightgown over her head. Anita then turned to collect the red dress. Olivia had pulled the nightgown over her head and became caught inside. "Anita," she gasped from inside the fabric.

Anita turned and her eyes went wide. She giggled quietly as she pulled the dress down until Olivia's head was free. But Olivia wasn't smiling. Tears now streaked down her round cheeks. "Sweetheart, why are you crying?" Anita asked, wiping the tears away from the child's face.

"Because I'm angry. My mother doesn't like me at all. That's why I hate her. She doesn't love me Anita," Olivia cried. "She's never loved me."

Anita sat down on the side of the bed, taking Olivia's hands into her own. "Now listen Olivia," she said sternly. "Your mother loves you very much."

"Well she doesn't show it," Olivia whimpered.

Olivia twisted a piece of hair around her finger and Anita took it from her, braiding her hair back behind her head in one long braid. The room turned silent. The only thing I could hear was Olivia's sniffling and Anita's movements. When she was done braiding, Anita slowly tied a ribbon to the child's hair and let the long braid fall back. She moved off of the bed and the springs squeaked.

"Don't go," Olivia begged, her voice hoarse.

Anita sighed deeply and nodded. She walked over to Olivia and patted the bed. The young girl lay back and Anita tucked her under the blankets. Olivia shut her eyes and she curled up, pressing her folded hands beneath her head. She looked peaceful as she slept. A young girl should not have so much stress in her life. I'd only seen a small part of this first life, and already I was exhausted.

"Tell me," I whispered, not even turning to look at Thyme who I knew was still standing there.

"Tell you what?" she questioned, her voice more serious than before.

I tiptoed over to the bed, even though Olivia couldn't hear me. I sat beside her and placed my hand on her head. "I'm her, aren't I?" I murmured. "I'm Olivia?"

My hand went right through Olivia's head and she didn't feel me at all. I couldn't feel her either. I simply closed my eyes and pretended that I was the little girl wrapped up in the blankets. I didn't have to pretend though. I had been her.

"When do I get to the good part?" I questioned, standing and turning back to Thyme.

She just shrugged and wore that same sly smile. I looked away. The room was illuminated by the moonlight from outside. "So I have the remote?"

"Yes," Thyme answered. "It's up to you to choose what to do with it."

I turned to face her, but she was gone and I was left alone in the room with people who didn't even know I was there. But the truth was, I wasn't really there. I was dead. I closed my eyes and took a deep breath, and when I opened them, the dark scene of the bedroom was gone, replaced by daylight. There was a slight spinning in my head.

Flowers

"The flowers are beautiful at this time of year," Anita said as Olivia ran out into an open field.

It must have been the day after the opera, because she was still in her blue nightgown. Olivia grabbed Anita's hand and pulled her along, running and spinning through the flowers. At first, Anita just stumbled, but then she let go and ran alongside Olivia. The flowers spun by in warm, beautiful blasts of color. Olivia continued to spin until she felt dizzy and fell back into the flowers. "I feel as if I am a bird," she said and Anita laughed, catching her breath and sinking down next to her.

"I feel as if I am old," Anita teased, and I laughed while Olivia did, too.

Thyme was nowhere in sight, and I didn't care. I wanted to run through the flowers too, and hold onto Anita's hand as tightly as I could. Olivia carefully plucked a sunflower, and handed it to Anita. "How lovely," Anita said, holding her hand over her heart with just enough emotion to make the child laugh freely.

Olivia's eyes changed slightly. "Why aren't you my mom?" she asked honestly.

This question seemed to take Olivia by surprise. "Because God gave you to your mother, who loves you very much."

Olivia looked into the distance. "I'd rather you be my mama. You feel like one. My mother doesn't even love me. But I know you do."

There were unshed tears in Anita's eyes. "I do love you, child," she said. "But I'm not your mother."

"Yes you are," Olivia whispered, so quietly that Anita probably didn't even hear.

I blinked.

First Meeting

Dawn awakened the world and sent light cascading through the room. The formerly light pink walls were now white. I could stomach this color much more than I could the pink. The rocking chair was now gone and replaced with a desk and a wooden chair. Pencils, paper, and books were scattered across the desk. The pink quilt was now light blue.

"Olivia!" an annoyingly high-pitched voice yelled as the door to the bedroom slammed open.

I jumped from the sudden sound. A young girl about sixteen or seventeen rushed inside. Her hair was very long, falling all the way down to her waist in a braid. She wore dark three-quarter pants that just reached her knees, the type of knickers that men wore. She was covered from head to toe in mud.

"Olivia!" the voice yelled again.

"What Mama?" Olivia shrieked as she rushed over to her bed and grabbed a bag with a hanger sticking out of it.

"We have to leave *now!*" Julia's cranky voice demanded. "The car is waiting!"

"I know! Give me one second!"

Olivia yanked the zipper down the bag, revealing a long, handmade gown. It was a deep blue and had a black ribbon around the waist. She made a face of disgust as she pulled it from the bag and began to pull off her mud-covered clothes. She tossed them into her closet, not caring where they landed. Her skin was tanned from being outside so often.

Footsteps came up the stairs as Olivia pulled on her dress and struggled to zip up the back, catching her hair in the zipper. She hissed with pain and readjusted before zipping it again, then ran to retrieve black dress shoes which she awkwardly shoved her feet into, hopping around the room. There was a loud knock at the door before the handle was twisted loudly. "Let me in, Olivia!" Julia commanded. "Why is your door locked?"

"Give me one second!" Olivia shouted.

She pulled her hair from the braid and forced a comb through the waves, cringing as she hit knots. She applied red lipstick, messily getting some on her chin. As she stared in the mirror, she stomped her foot against the floor as she licked her finger and wiped the dirt from her cheek. She quickly began to dab some powder onto her face, covering a scratch. Some powder fell onto her dress. She cussed under her breath.

"What on earth are you doing?" Julia demanded, pounding on the door once again.

Olivia quickly rubbed out the makeup from her dress. Her green eyes were big and bright and her hair fell down her back in beautiful waves. She cringed at how she looked and stomped over to the door, unlocking it and yanking it open right as Julia raised her fist to knock again.

Julia froze and let her hands drop to her side. Her hair was done up in something that resembled a bird's nest. She wore a sleeveless black dress that flowed to her ankles. Her makeup was overdone, her eye shadow a dark blue and her lipstick a deep red. She frowned and looked Olivia over once. She motioned at the bottom of her dress and Olivia sighed and pulled it up above her ankles.

"No stockings?" Julia questioned, her voice emotionless. Olivia scowled. "Well, it will have to do. We are already late as it is. Let's go."

The scene changed and I was watching as Julia and Olivia entered a large room. It was filled with people dressed in fancy clothing of the early 1900s. So many ruffles and frills made Olivia cringe. The room was adorned in chandeliers and candles and expensive silver.

Violins and flutes graced the air with their sound.

Henry was close behind Julia. She locked arms with him as he caught up to her and he led her to the middle of the ballroom. Olivia looked for an escape, finding comfort in a cushion-covered bench in a coatroom. There were only a few candles in there.

"Good evening," a boy said, making Olivia jump. He looked very familiar to me. "I'm sorry. Did I startle you?"

"Not at all," Olivia said, re-plastering the blank look on her face.

"Is this the new place to pass the time?" the boy chuckled, hanging a long, black coat in the back of the closet.

Olivia looked up, her gaze fixing on his. "It's better in here than out there."

The light of the candles flickered and I got a good look at him. He was tall and blond, eyes a deep blue. "Patrick," he said, extending a hand.

The look on Olivia's face continued to stay blank, but against her better judgment, she took his hand, shook it, and released it. "How do you do?" Olivia asked, pretending to be polite.

"I didn't quite catch your name," Patrick said, keeping his eyes fixed on hers.

"It's Mercy," Olivia lied smoothly.

Patrick gave her a charming smile. "Well Mercy, can you answer a question for me? It's bothering me very much."

Olivia shrugged, a sly smile tugging at the corner of her lips. "I've nothing more interesting to do."

Patrick chuckled deeply. His voice was like music. It just flowed. "What is a stunning girl like you doing in a room meant for hanging coats?"

Olivia looked around her, pretending to be completely baffled as she touched her hand to her chest. "Oh, did you mean me? The lighting must be awful in here if you think *I* am stunning. I am merely a girl."

"But there is nothing mere about you. Your very being takes my breath away," Patrick said dreamily.

He sat down next to Olivia and she automatically leaned away. "Are you trying to charm me?" she demanded.

Patrick gave her a crooked smile. I was as charmed as I could get, but I couldn't say the same for Olivia. I leaned back against a wall. It didn't support me in the least and I fell right down, landing backwards in a gold hallway. I quickly stood up and pushed back into the room where Patrick had managed to get closer to Olivia.

"I was simply being nice," he was saying.

"I don't even know you," Olivia said, narrowing her eyes.

Patrick ignored her stubbornness and responded, "You know, you never *did* answer my initial question. Why are you in here?"

"Because," Olivia finally gave in, standing from the bench and smoothing the front of her dress. "People don't usually want to talk to me in *there*."

And with that, she left the room. Patrick stared after her with shock, and a hint of admiration spread across his face. He didn't even know her real name, and already, she had him wrapped around her finger.

Olivia headed straight through the crowd, squeezing in tightly so she wouldn't be seen. She found Henry. He was talking to another man with a hairy mustache and an oddly shaved beard. "Father," Olivia said, taking his elbow into her hand.

"Ah, Olivia." Henry smiled. "I would like you to meet Carlson Minster."

Olivia stiffened at the name and immediately plastered on a polite smile. "Mr. Minster," Olivia said, holding out her hand. "It is an honor to meet you."

Mr. Minster took her hand and kissed it. "Same to you," he responded, his voice gruff and raspy.

His last name seemed to sit in my head. I knew I'd heard it before.

"Can you imagine?" Mr. Minster chuckled. "We could all be family."

Olivia nodded her head and continued to grin, yet it never reached her eyes. "Indeed," Olivia sighed.

Mr. Minster excused himself to get a drink. Olivia turned to her father. "I want to leave," she insisted.

"Olivia," Henry whispered, leaning so closely I could barely hear it. I imagined turning up the volume, and just like that, I could hear them. Thyme was right. I really could control this. I was the remote. "We must impress this family. You could be marrying their son one day. Isn't that what you want?"

Olivia scowled. "Yes father. That's *exactly* what I want. I would love to tie my life to someone else's. I'll share my belongings with him too. Nothing will be sacred and nothing will be just mine. I will have to confirm everything in my life with another."

Henry placed his hand on Olivia's shoulder. "Marriage is so much more than that, darling. It will keep you safe and secure all of your life. It is completely worth it. When I first met your mother, I was skeptical as well. And look at us now."

"Why yes," Olivia said sarcastically. "Because you adore her *so* much."

"Olivia. You watch your tongue!" her father warned.

She skulked away toward the coat closet, dragging her dress along the ground without caring whether it tore, but before she could reach it, a hand grasped onto her own and yanked her through the crowd. "Mama!" Olivia gasped. "What on earth?"

"I want you to meet the Minsters," Julia commanded,

her voice overly peppy and high, her words slurred. She was drunk.

"We've been introduced," Olivia insisted as they stopped at a table. "Miriam," Julia said to a heavy woman with long blond hair who sat before her. "This is Olivia."

"Oh!" Miriam stood at once. "What a pleasure. She's a beauty."

"I'm right here," Olivia muttered to herself.

"You will have to meet my son. He could be your future husband, dear. Wait right here."

Olivia's eyes widened and she tries to stop her. It was then that Patrick emerged from the crowd and stopped before her. "We meet again," he said.

"What could you possibly want?" Olivia hissed.

"Olivia!" Julia scolded and something seemed to dawn on her daughter.

"You are *the* Patrick?" Olivia gaped. "Pardon my manners."

"I thought your name was Mercy."

"Well, then, you misunderstood," Olivia insisted as the music changed.

Patrick went along with it, catching onto the whole game. "Alright. Well, since you may be my future wife, what do you say to a dance?" He extended his hand to her.

"I'm not much of a dancer," Olivia started, but Julia pushed her in the back and she stumbled towards Patrick.

He caught her and took her hand. Olivia let out a huff of breath and followed Patrick to the dance floor. When they reached it, Patrick placed a hand on Olivia's waist and she placed a hand on his shoulder. Their free hands clasped together and they began to sway back and forth. "So tell me," Patrick began. "Why lie about your name? Why not tell me what your name really is?"

"Because my name is not for your knowing. Why should I share it?"

"Why not?"

Olivia narrowed her eyes. Her red hair fell into her face and Patrick released her hand to move her hair out of her eyes. Olivia said nothing. She just continued to sway, re-clasping her hand with Patrick's.

"Why Mercy?" he asked suddenly.

"Excuse me?"

"Of all names, why did Mercy come to mind?"

"You *do* ask a lot of questions," Olivia snapped, rolling her eyes. "I will answer one more and this is the last. I chose Mercy because I've always loved it. It implies power. It gives a name meaning."

"But I thought you were the exact opposite of that," Patrick mused.

"I am. But it was the first name that came to mind. And sometimes it is nice to be somebody else for a change."

"But why?"

"I said no more questions," Olivia smirked.

"If I would've believed that that was my last question, I would've chosen more wisely."

"It is too late for that now, isn't it?"

Without warning, Patrick spun Olivia. She let out a tiny squeak as she twirled and he caught her much closer than they were before. Their faces were inches apart. "For somebody who can't dance," he whispered, his lips directly next to her ear, "you seem to know what you are doing."

Olivia's breath caught in her throat and she stepped back. "I should go," she got out.

Patrick's disappointment was obvious. "But why?"

"I must go," Olivia repeated, more firmly this time.

She turned and pushed her way through the crowd once again, oblivious of everyone around her as she fled toward the safety of the coat closet. One man didn't realize she was there and accidentally knocked her over before she could reach it. She fell to the floor, landing on her arm and cringing. I felt a dull pain in my own arm. It faded quickly. Olivia didn't stay there long before she stood and began to walk again.

"Father, I want to leave right now," Olivia insisted when she found him conversing with an old woman.

"Pardon me," Henry said politely to the old woman and stepped around her to Olivia. "We've already discussed this," he hissed at her. "I've had enough, Olivia. Please go and at least *try* to make yourself pleasant."

"No," Olivia persisted. "I've hurt myself."

"Where?" Henry asked, immediately concerned.

"My wrist," Olivia said, holding her arm straight out to him.

He took it gingerly into his own hand and shook his head. "There is no swelling or bruising-"

"Oh, but it *hurts*! I twisted it. It could be a sprain. I would like to go home at once." She batted her eyelashes at him and clenched her other fist at her side.

"Olivia! Henry!" Julia shouted, making her way over to them. "I've been looking everywhere for the two of you. When I realized you weren't with Patrick any longer, I wasn't sure what had happened to you."

She swayed a bit on her feet and Henry turned his attention away from Olivia to take Julia's drink from her hand and set it on the table next to him. "Olivia has hurt herself," he explained and it took Julia a long moment before she became concerned.

"Oh my... that's not good is it? Do you think you will be alright for the rest of the night?" Julia slurred.

"No!" Olivia insisted. "Mama..."

"Oh but you look alright."

"Mother!" Olivia hissed. "I would like to leave at once. I danced with Patrick and I met his family. I made small talk. I am *hurt* now!"

"I see that," Julia muttered. "Henry, go get our coats.

We will be waiting in the front."

"Of course," Henry said, and Olivia narrowed her eyes as she followed Julia out.

I quickly chased after them. The hallway led to a large, circular entryway filled with statues and vases that were all clearly made by hand. Olivia kept her head down, staring at her wrist, which now looked slightly bruised. "What did you think of Patrick?" Julia questioned, hope in her voice.

"He was... interesting," Olivia groaned.

"I absolutely approve of the Minsters. I definitely see a marriage in your future. Not only do they have *a lot* of money, but they aren't *completely* boring," Julia stammered.

"Do I get any say in this?" Olivia asked with annoyance clearly in her eyes.

"In what?" Julia asked as Henry walked out with their coats, and Olivia dropped the topic.

I was tired of staring at Julia's drunken face and I fast forwarded through the night with a blink of my eyes. I was dizzy when it stopped. I was back in Olivia's dark bedroom with a single candle burning on the bedside table. Anita was holding Olivia's hand in her own and it was bandaged and being iced at the moment. "It's not as bad as I made it seem," Olivia finally admitted and pulled her hand away. "I just needed to get out of there."

Anita looked much older. Her hair was long and white and it hung down behind her. "Why would you lie about hurting yourself, dear?" she asked, sounding concerned.

"I didn't *completely* lie. I actually did land on my wrist. But it's really just a bruise." Olivia played with a piece of the bandage on her wrist, refusing to look up at Anita. "Don't tell my parents."

Anita smiled wryly. "I never tell your secrets dear," she sighed and ran her fingers through Olivia's hair. "How was this Patrick fellow?"

"Full of himself. Nothing special. But my parents don't quite agree," Olivia mumbled, turning onto her side and pulling her blankets tightly up to her chest. "My mother is inviting them all for dinner. You can see for yourself."

"Was he at least good looking?" Anita pressed.

Olivia said nothing. She just looked up from under her thick eyelashes and stared at Anita. The corners of her lips curled up and Anita laughed quietly. "That's the only thing I like about him," Olivia admitted. "Sometimes I wish I could just run away."

"Olivia?"

"I would take you with me," Olivia whispered. "You care for me. I know my father sort of does. My mother does not at all. But where would I go? I'm just a girl who's been spoiled rotten. I'd never make it past the garden."

Anita sighed heavily and patted Olivia on the head. "Get some sleep, dear," she said.

"Stay," Olivia yawned and pulled the blankets tighter around her.

Anita sat down in a chair in the corner of the room and watched Olivia. I could see tears in her old, worn eyes. Olivia was sound asleep in minutes, tired from the long night. Anita carefully stood and made her way across the room. She pulled the blanket up higher over Olivia's shoulders to cover her bare skin. "Sleep well," she whispered, and kissed her head before blowing out the candle and leaving me in the darkness of the room with Olivia.

I could hear odd sounds circulating through the room. I stood up, trying to find running water, but finding nothing other than Olivia. I walked in circles, finally giving up and dropping to the ground, closing my eyes.

I could see an ocean behind my eyelids. I was walking towards it. It was beautiful. The waves rolled and sparkled under the sun. The water was so blue that it was surreal.

The sun shone high in the sky, reflecting gold rays onto the crystal surface. My fingers reached forwards, just about to touch the diamond-like water when it disappeared from under me and the world faded to darkness and I was falling.

My eyes shot open and Olivia sat up in bed, gasping for air. I did the same. If my heart was still beating, it would be racing at the moment. The fact that I couldn't hear my pulse in my ears made me feel so fake and inhuman. I curled up quietly, needing to take a break from this craziness.

"Dreams are memories too," a voice said from next to me and I flung my arms out, striking Thyme and bringing her to the floor.

She fell back to the ground and her eyes widened. "Well that's a new reaction."

Olivia settled back in her bed and reached over to touch the wick of the candle, pulling her hand back when she realized that it was still warm and that Anita has just left. She slammed her eyes shut and tears welled up, staining her lashes.

"Where were you?" I whispered, standing from the ground to watch Olivia closer.

"You know," Thyme said, irritably. "You are not my only client. A lot of people die in one day."

"Really?" I hissed. "I'm so sick of this! Why can't I just get my memories back and go to heaven like *everybody else*?"

"Many people have to go through this!" Thyme hissed. "Some are satisfied with one life and they live it in their afterlife. You're much more difficult."

"Wait… there's more than one life?"

"Fast forward. I promise, it gets better. Go watch that dinner your mother is setting up. That story is very interesting," Thyme explained and I glowered.

"You already *know* what happens?"

Thyme shrugged. "I know everything, Jane Doe."

Dinner

I closed my eyes and the world spun and I was standing in Olivia's bedroom, watching as Anita helped her into a lovely, sky-blue dress that reached the floor. Anita pulled the strings in the back and they tightened until Olivia could barely breathe, and that's when Anita tied it. The sleeves of the dress just touched her shoulders, but they didn't fully cover them. Her back was visible through the ties in the dress. On her neck she wore a pearl necklace, and she had a set of pearl earrings on. "You are stunning," Anita assured her when she saw the worry in Olivia's eyes.

As Olivia turned, I saw that her hair was curled and it hung down over her shoulders. She was even wearing more makeup than just powder to cover a scratch. Anita smiled a vibrant smile and clapped her hands together. "Just wait until he sees you," she said.

Olivia looked worried and, instead of saying anything in response, she leaned forwards and took Anita into her arms. Anita was slightly surprised by this, but she hugged her back. "I don't want to be married," Olivia cried softly. "I just want to have fun. I don't want half my life to be half of his. I'm not meant for something like this."

"Oh dear," Anita sighed and pulled away. She patted the bed and Olivia sat down. Anita kneeled down in front of her. "Don't cry," she murmured, "you'll ruin your makeup."

Olivia looked down and her shoulders shook with sobs. "I don't love him. I don't even know him! Why should I be married to him?"

Anita touched the side of Olivia's face and wiped the tears away with her fingers. She fixed Olivia's makeup with the sleeve of her shirt. "You look at me," Anita said. "I don't agree with this and you and I both know that. But I can't control what your parents do. I am the nanny and nothing more than that. I don't get a say in anything except to tell you that you are special and beautiful."

Olivia took Anita's hand. "You're so much more than just the nanny to me."

Anita had tears in her eyes and she blinked them away. "I know dear. I know."

I closed my eyes and the world rushed around me and I was standing in a dining room. There was a large, wooden table that stretched through the room and a wooden case that held fine china. Julia was taking out plates and setting them at the table. Olivia blinked a few times as she entered the room. It wasn't very obvious that she had been crying. Her eyes were slightly red, but it just looked like she hadn't gotten enough sleep. She probably hadn't.

"Once again, you decide to wear blue," Julia sighed in defeat. "Can't you wear anything brighter? Look at what I'm wearing."

Julia's dress was long and red, and the sleeves just reach her elbows. Her hair was pulled back into a braid. She looked as if she was trying to dress up as a queen and failed miserably. Olivia said nothing. She took a seat at the table, and at that moment, there was a knock on the door.

"They're here!" Julia shouted, rushing into the other room. "Henry! Get in here! Anita, get the door!"

Olivia rolled her eyes and dug her nails into her palms. Moments later, Patrick, Miriam, and Mr. Minster were being ushered into the room. Patrick's hair was slicked back and he was wearing a black dress suit. He looked very handsome and I could barely help ogling him.

"Good evening," he murmured to Olivia.

She stood up politely and reached out her hand. Patrick bent over, took it and kissed it. As he looked up at her through his eyelashes, Olivia's breath caught in her throat, and she quickly yanked her hand away and flounced to her place at the table. Henry walked in at that moment and took a seat next to Olivia. Julia sat next to him. On the other side of the table, Patrick, Miriam, and Mr. Minster took their seats. Anita entered and Julia narrowed her eyes. "What is the *help* doing in here?" Miriam asked in an ugly tone.

"Mother," Patrick hissed quietly.

"She was just leaving," Julia said quickly, glaring at Anita who quickly left the room without a word. "She is serving the dinner."

"This is lovely Julia," Miriam said through her nose.

"Thank you." Julia forced her lips to curve up into a smile and Anita walked in to place the food in the middle of the table.

"Is that all?" Anita asked, her voice flat.

"Thank you Anita," Julia muttered with an edge to her voice. "That will be all."

I took a seat in a chair at the end of the table and I watched as the conversation became forced. "Yesterday Patrick was out hunting with his father. He shot a deer and skinned it himself."

Olivia began to take a bite of chicken, but froze and placed her fork down, folding her hands in her lap. "How lovely," she mumbled, her face twisted with disgust.

"Olivia has many talents as well. She can play the violin. She is very smart."

Olivia glared. "Mother, may I please be excused?"

Julia gaped at her. "Now?"

"Yes please. I need some air."

"No, of course not," Julia started when Patrick suddenly bolted straight out of his chair.

"I'll go with her," he said. "I'd like some time with her alone."

Julia hesitated for a long moment and then nodded. "Don't be too long. Come back before the sun fully sets."

Patrick held his arm out to Olivia and she reluctantly took it and they walked out the front door. I followed them.

Olivia sighed with relief as the nighttime air hits her. She pulled her arm from Patrick's, but she stayed close to him.

"So you hunt," she said, starting conversation.

Patrick nodded. "It's a way to pass the time."

"But you're taking away lives."

Patrick turned to her. "We have to eat, Olivia. That chicken at dinner; you ate it with no problem."

"Well that's different. I didn't *kill* it."

"Somebody did," Patrick pointed out. "It was probably that girl Anita."

"Yes, I know it was. It's her job. But doesn't it upset you? You raise these poor animals. You feed them. You name them. You give them a home. And for what? To chop off their heads and call them dinner." She motioned to the chicken coop that they passed. The birds jumped toward her but she walked right past them.

"I suppose," Patrick sighed. "But I don't think of it much, and I don't name the animals I hunt."

Olivia stared at her feet. "I don't want to marry you," she whispered as they started to head downhill.

"I know," Patrick said simply, and took her arm again.

This time, she didn't pull her arm back. They walked into the forest where a fence surrounded their land. Olivia watched Patrick's arm the whole time, and she didn't pull back until they reached the fence. She leaned against it, shutting her eyes. "I used to hide out here all day when I was a young girl. I could avoid my mother that way."

"Why avoid her?" Patrick questioned and Olivia smiled, though her eyes were still closed.

"Once again with the questions," Olivia teased and then her smile faded. "My mother has never seen me for who I truly was. She saw me as the girl who the family's fate rests upon. But nobody fully understands me. Not even Anita. She tries though."

"I think I get you," Patrick started and Olivia laughed

humorlessly. "I'm serious."

"Well then, off you go. Tell me," Olivia insisted with sarcasm in her tone. "Tell me all about me."

"You are a girl," Patrick said, "who is much stronger than people see. You aren't weak, but people don't understand that. You aren't like the other girls. You aren't interested in money and objects. You're more than that." He touched her face lightly and she didn't object as her eyes fixed on his. His voice dropped to a whisper when he spoke again. "You don't want to marry because you are told to. You want to marry for love."

Olivia's eyes didn't move from Patrick's face. "And how do you know that?"

"Because I am the same way," Patrick admitted.

Olivia blinked once and whispered, "But you want to marry me."

Patrick shook his head. "No. You have it all wrong. I simply want to get to know you."

Their faces were inches apart, and without another word, Olivia closed the distance and pressed her lips against his. It was very quick and she pulled back immediately, shocked at what she had done. She covered her mouth with her hands as Patrick's eyes went wide. "I'm sorry. I didn't mean to—"

Olivia was cut off as Patrick pulled her right back to him and kissed her again. The sun was barely visible anymore behind them and darkness encased the world. Olivia pulled away for a moment and whispered. "This still doesn't mean you know me."

Patrick smirked and pecked her on the lips. "Yet," he said, and they kissed again.

It didn't last long and finally Olivia stopped it. "We should go back," she reminded him.

"So soon?" Patrick pouted and Olivia giggled, pulling him by the hand.

"Aren't they adorable?" Thyme said from behind me and I didn't even flinch.

"Yep," I muttered and closed my eyes.

Proposal

"Patrick's here!" called a shrill voice, and I groaned as I landed on the floor and my head continued to spin.

You would think that I would be used to the spinning by now. But it just seemed to get worse and worse. If I wasn't dead, I would have bet that I was about to throw up.

"Coming Mama," Olivia said softly, walking into the kitchen.

Something was different about her. Her red hair was pulled back into a braid. She wore a white dress that ended above her ankles and had long sleeves. "There you are," Julia said. "And you look lovely."

"Thank you Mother," Olivia whispered and seemed to walk on air as she exited the house through the front door.

Patrick was waiting on the steps outside for her, and the second the door closed behind her, the facade ends and her smile turned to a smirk as she rolled her eyes. "You look beautiful as always," Patrick chuckled and Olivia sighed, pulling him behind the house.

"Thank you." She untied her dress and my eyes went wide until she removed it to reveal a long sleeve shirt and knickers. "Where are we going today?" she questioned, folding the dress and slipping it behind a bush.

"Do you really want to leave it there?"

"Anita will take care of it," Olivia explained. "Now answer my question."

"We are going for a walk."

"A walk?" Olivia questioned with curiosity. "To where?"

"The lake of course."

It's then that I got a close up of Olivia's face. She looked slightly older, maybe nineteen or twenty. She was still beautiful. She had grown a lot since I last saw her.

"The lake!" Olivia laughed as Patrick took her hand and pulled her along.

I had no patience to follow them through the forest so I shut my eyes and fast forwarded to the lake. The dizziness wasn't as bad this time. Not as much time had passed. It had only been about an hour.

"Finally," Olivia sighed, walking through the trees and stopping in front of a huge, slightly green lake.

The sun shone brightly, bouncing off of the lake in a beautifully bright way. Olivia shielded her eyes and sweat was beading on her forehead. A duck waddled past them and Olivia giggled. "Okay. We are at the lake. Now what?"

"Now…" Patrick started and stripped off his shirt. "We swim."

Olivia gasped. "Wait," she started and he pulled off his pants and stood there in only his underwear.

I noticed, with careful scrutiny, that he had six pack abs and his arm muscles were huge. He laughed quietly and turned to dive into the lake.

"Patrick!" Olivia squealed. He resurfaced and his blond hair stuck to his forehead.

"Are you coming in or not?" he called.

Olivia backed away slightly and stared down at the clothes she wore that would usually be worn by men. She unbuttoned the top of her shirt and then froze. "I don't know," she started.

"Have a little fun," Patrick called.

"But if we are caught…"

"We won't be!" Patrick promised.

Olivia carefully unbuttoned the rest of the shirt to reveal an undershirt and then she pulled her pants down. Her underwear was much like shorts. Unlike Patrick, she managed to stay rather covered and then she dipped her foot into the water. "It's warm."

Patrick disappeared under the water, and reappeared, grabbing her foot and yanking her forwards. She screamed in shock and was engulfed by the water. Seconds later, she pulled herself above the water and coughed, spitting it from her mouth. Patrick came up from behind her, laughing. Olivia looked like a wet cat and she shoved Patrick. She had trouble staying above water and she clung to him. "Hey, relax," he said, pulling her back towards the shore where the mud became a ramp.

"I'm not the best swimmer," Olivia admitted, hugging Patrick tightly and refusing to let go.

Patrick fell back against the mud, taking Olivia with him. There were tears in her eyes and her nails dug into his skin. "Easy," Patrick whispered. "It's okay. You're alright. I've got you."

Olivia hid her face against his neck. "How humiliating," she mumbled. Her shirt clung to her tightly and her hair stuck to her skin. The tears were blinked away and she sighed into his grip. "Don't let me go. Not ever."

"Never," Patrick promised, laying further into the mud. "Will you marry me?"

Olivia slowly leaned back and her knees found the mud as she sat up in his lap. "I-I can't," Olivia whispered and broke into a sob. "I can't marry you." Patrick's face fell and Olivia was quick to explain. "No, no. It's not that I don't want to be with you. I just can't give into what my parents want. I don't want them to have their way, to think they control my life. And marriage is very permanent."

"Don't you think what we have is permanent?"

"I mean… I do but…"

"Don't marry me because they want you to. Marry me because *you* want to."

Patrick's eyes looked desperate. "Okay," Olivia suddenly whispered.

Patrick's eyes widened. "Yes?" he gasped.

Olivia pressed her lips together and nodded and tears started to run down her cheeks and she laughed through her tears. "Yes!"

Strike One

"You look beautiful!" Julia exclaimed, and her figure came into view as the spinning wore off.

Olivia's hair was a mess. She wore a long, white dress. It was low cut and the sleeves flowed out at her elbows. She looked miserable as she turned away from the mirror in a room that I didn't recognize.

"I don't feel like it," she muttered.

Miriam walked up behind her and, without warning, began to yank the knots out of Olivia's hair with a brush. She quickly pulled herself free and ran down the hall and out the front door. "Olivia!" Julia yelled and Miriam stood there with her mouth wide open.

Olivia held up the bottom of her dress as she ran across a field and right into Patrick. He caught her and she just let him hold her as she glared.

"I hate this!" she shrieked against him. "They are dressing me like a doll. This was supposed to be the beginning of our lives together, and yet I still feel as if I am just losing my freedom."

"Is that really all this is to you?" Patrick asked, his voice on edge. "You still feel forced? As if you are losing your freedom?"

Olivia turned quickly. "Leave me alone."

He followed after her. "No! You are my fiancé. We should make decisions together. This marriage is not forced. We have something special. We have love."

Olivia grabbed his hand suddenly. "Then run away with me."

"W-what?"

"Let's get out of here and never look back," Olivia said hopefully. "Please Patrick."

Patrick slowly pulled his hand away. "Olivia, I love

you. But I can't leave my family."

"Oh, you mean your mother who doesn't give a damn about you and your father who only ever gets joy out of a good drink?"

She was cut off as Patrick's hand collided with her face, forcing it to the side. She gasped and I gasped at the same time in pure shock. My face hurt.

"I-I didn't mean to..." Olivia trailed off, her lip quivering and Patrick backed up, appalled.

"I don't know what happened," he stammered, reaching towards her. Olivia automatically backed away. "No," Patrick stopped her. "Don't be afraid of me. I didn't mean to hit you. It's just... they are my parents."

Olivia nodded slowly. "I'll see you tomorrow at the wedding," she whispered and ran back towards the house.

Wedding

"Your father will be waiting outside the door," Julia said as I fast forwarded into the room.

"Okay," Olivia whispered, turning.

Her face was covered in makeup and her hair was pulled back into an extravagant braid. She wore the same white dress as yesterday, but she seemed to carry it better today. Julia's purple gown trailed after her as she left the room and closed the door. Anita snuck in then.

"Anita!" Olivia threw her arms around her. "They should have let you come! I want you here, at my wedding."

"You'll do great," Anita said, slowly pushing her away. "You look gorgeous. You are with the man you love. You don't need me here to establish that."

"Yes I do. No matter what, Anita, you will always be my real mother." Olivia fought back tears and Anita did as well. "Patrick hit me yesterday," Olivia whispered, touching the bruise on her cheek that she must have covered with powder.

Anita's eyes went wide, and before she could respond, Olivia turned and left the room, wiping her tears. She met Henry outside the door. He looked very handsome, and it was not just because of his suit or the way his thinning grey hair had been brushed back. It was the genuine smile that he wore on his face.

"Hello darling," Henry said, and Olivia took his arm. "Ready to be married?"

"As I'll ever be." Henry hugged her close before walking her down the aisle to where Patrick was waiting for her at the altar.

I took a seat in the audience and watched as Olivia held her head high and proud, standing across from him. She was fearless. Patrick smiled at her with guilt in his eyes and she nodded back. It was as if she was in an arranged marriage once again, marrying a stranger with pride. Her love was hidden behind her expressionless gaze.

The priest began to talk. A figure sat in the empty seat beside me in the back row and I turned to see Thyme. "Don't you just love weddings?" she said.

I rolled my eyes. "Apparently not," I said, motioning to Olivia.

For a moment, as she was asked to agree to the marriage, there was a hint of feeling in her eyes—was it sorrow? Regret?—but just as quickly, it faded away.

"I do," she said in a strong voice.

I couldn't take watching this anymore and I blinked, allowing myself to reappear later in the night. Thyme still stood with me and I watched as Olivia climbed into a car with Patrick close behind her. People cheered for them until the door was shut. I walked straight through the door and into the car, watching them.

Olivia leaned away, sitting straight again. The driver got into the front and started the car. He was smoking a cigar. Patrick looked over at Olivia and touched her cheek lightly. She didn't budge, just kept her eyes straight ahead. Her lip quivered slightly.

In silence, Patrick wrapped his arm around Olivia and pulled her close. They didn't talk. They just held on until the night wrapped around them.

Strike Two

My head was spinning so hard it hurt and I doubled over, cradling it in my hands. The dizziness took forever to subside. My vision finally cleared and I found Henry and Anita waiting desperately in front of the door, practically bouncing up and down. Just by looking at Anita's face, I could tell that years had passed. Her hair was white and flimsy looking. Her face was covered in wrinkles, and she had trouble standing straight. Henry's hair was graying and a lot of it was gone. Julia was attempting to cover her wrinkles with tons of makeup. Anita coughed dryly as she waited.

"There she is!" Henry announced, throwing the door open as a car pulled into the driveway.

Olivia slowly stepped out with a renewed smile on her face and Patrick walked out after her. Their hands entwined immediately.

Olivia ran forwards and threw her arms around Anita, having gone right past her parents. Mr. Minster and Miriam appeared in the doorway as well, and Patrick hugged them both. Olivia then hugged her parents quickly, barely even touching her mother.

A car pulled up into the driveway and a tall, curvy, blond woman climbed out. She saw Patrick and Olivia and smiled. The second I saw her, I froze. I knew her. I could feel it. Wait, wasn't she at the wedding? I already loved her as a sister. But she was not my sister. Was she?

"Hello brother!" the girl called and Patrick stared with his mouth wide open.

"Emily?" Miriam whispered and Mr. Minster dropped his cigar.

"Mother. Father," she greeted, nodding at both of them. "Olivia, dear!"

"Where have you been?" Miriam exclaimed, and Patrick quickly hugged Emily before he allowed the parents to talk.

"She's back?" Olivia whispered as Patrick pulled her into the house, but he just shook his head and left.

"If you want to get to the good part, fast-forward a bit," Thyme said and I turned to face her.

"Fancy seeing you here."

"Well you appear to have gotten the hang of things. I have to check up on some stuff."

"Like what?"

"Oh just fast-forward," Thyme insisted and I did.

There was barely any spinning. Patrick pulled Olivia up onto a hill in the middle of a field. "Where are we going?" Olivia giggled, stumbling along with him. "Patrick?"

"Love, please trust me," Patrick pleaded.

The top of the hill was revealed and a picnic blanket was spread across it with lit candles, Champagne, dinner, oh, and Emily.

"Sister!" Emily exclaimed, standing to hug Olivia tightly. She whispered something and I had to rewind and turn up the volume to hear her say, "How has the anger been lately?"

Olivia didn't respond, but there was sadness in her eyes. "Emily!" Olivia squealed, ignoring her question. "Where have you been?"

"Starting to sound like mother much?" Emily giggled and pulled a cigarette from her pocket, lighting it. The Champaign bottle was half empty; she had already had a few drinks. "But to answer your question," she started between inhales of smoke. "I traveled the world. I saw America. Do you know what America has? Freedom dear. No parents. It is the land of the free for a reason, baby. You, me, and Pat over here, we all belong in America."

Olivia turned to Patrick, a huge smile on her face and

hope in her eyes. "No," Patrick said simply.

"Oh and they have the most beautiful beaches. I could teach you to swim. To really swim. Can you imagine us in America?"

I was slightly surprised, quickly realizing that I had skipped a long period of time, and that these two were friends. Suddenly, this made total sense to me. Of course! I loved Emily! I remembered her!

"Emily, that is enough," Patrick warned.

"Oh brother, you need to learn to relax." Emily inhaled deeply and exhaled the smoke through her nostrils. She smiled and I saw that she had crooked teeth. "What do you say Pat?"

"Absolutely not."

Olivia was staring at her feet. "Of course," she says bitterly.

"Are you saying you want to leave?"

"I would just like to discuss things with you before you automatically say no!" Olivia picked up the Champagne bottle and drank straight from it, placing it back onto the ground.

"Olivia. Some manners?" Patrick reminded her.

"I hate being under the control of someone else. I despise it. Patrick, sweetie, can we simply talk about this?"

"Em," Patrick said, turning to his wild sister. "May we have a moment?"

"Oh the drama of dramatics," Emily responded drunkenly before staggering down the hill.

"Alright," Patrick hissed. "What now? You still want to leave? And to America of all places?"

"No," Emily sighed. "Not America. It's just that... I've been here my whole life. And don't you remember our honeymoon? I was so happy! It was somewhere new and different. And we always come back here. Please, can we just leave?"

44

"No! I don't want to leave my family!" Patrick insisted.

"But I don't want to stay!" Olivia protested and Patrick shoved her.

She fell back against the ground. "You promised it would never happen again," Olivia whispered and then cried, "*You swore!*"

"Please calm down," Patrick pleaded, fear ruining his easy stature. "Just stop it already!"

Olivia pushed herself up from the ground and fury narrowed her eyes. Patrick reached for her arm, trying to stop her. "Don't touch me!" Olivia shrieked.

Patrick backed away. "You asked for it," he said quietly, and as Olivia backed slowly away, he lifted the Champagne and threw it as hard as he could. "*You asked for it!*"

He shouted loudly as it narrowly missed Olivia and shattered to the ground. A piece of glass impaled her arm. Blood slowly dripped down her skin and she just stood there, staring at it. My arm began to throb. She slowly looked up at Patrick, who was frozen in shock, and she turned and fled as fast as she could manage through the forest.

Patrick watched with a wild look in his eyes, and then he dropped to the ground. It seemed as if what he just did hit him all at once. He closed his eyes and tears ran down his face as his wife continued to run off into the distance.

Run

When I caught my balance, I watched as Julia paced the hallways and Henry sat on the couch in the living room, hiding his face in his hands. An older man, thin and bony with grey hair, descended the steps. He had bent glasses resting on his nose. Every few seconds, he turned his face into his elbow and coughed as if he is hacking up a lung. Henry stood immediately and his eyes were bloodshot. Julia just watched without saying a word. The old man shook his head and coughed loudly once more. "There was nothing to be done. Pneumonia has no mercy. She's gone."

Julia showed no emotion and Henry sat down, staring out the window with tears in his eyes. "Is Olivia dead?" I gasped, knowing Thyme was always close by.

"Keep watching," she whispered, and her voice was melancholy.

"But if she's dead… why am I still here?"

I closed my eyes, trying to imagine death. First I felt my lungs closing. And then the soft fabric of sheets. And finally, rain and weakness.

"It's not her," I suddenly realized. "It's—"

"*Anita!*" Olivia screamed, running through the front door.

She ran into the den and stopped when she saw the old man and her parents with their distraught faces. "Where is Anita?" Olivia demanded as tears ran down her cheeks and blood dripped down her arm. "Mother? Father?"

I could feel my own throat contracting at the thought of the loss. "Darling," Henry said slowly, standing from the sofa. His voice cracked. "Anita has been very ill," he started.

It seemed to hit Olivia then. "No," she whispered.

"There was nothing he could do for her," Julia cut in.

"No!"

"She had pneumonia," Henry sighed. "I'm so sorry. Anita's gone."

Olivia looked back and forth between the two of them and then rushed up the steps screaming, "Anita! *Anita!*"

I followed after her. "No!" Thyme called. "You really shouldn't see this again!"

The word *again* hit somewhere in the back of my mind, but I let it pass by. When Olivia reached Anita's small, plain, white room, she stopped, seeing the blankets covering the shape of a body. "No," Olivia sobbed, falling to the ground. "*No!*"

She was kneeling before the bed and she began to sing the song that Anita would sing to her as a child.

"Sweet little girl, please don't cry.

It's time to rest now. Close your eyes..."

She broke off into sobs.

"Olivia!" Henry was shouting, running up the steps.

Julia wasn't far behind. "Olivia please!" she yelled, sounding worried about her daughter for the first time in her life.

Olivia slowly looked up at the window at the side of the room, and when I blinked, I was no longer there.

Ocean

The darkness prevented the dizziness from affecting my vision too much. At first I saw something moving and sparkling. As my vision adjusted, I saw that I was on a deserted beach, the moon shining high over the ocean. The waves seemed to have a magnetic pull and they were tugged back and forth towards the moon and then over the sand. A woman stood in the middle of all of it, her red hair glowing in the moonlight.

Olivia.

Her hair was blown back by the breeze and the waves washed up and sank back down around her bare feet. Her breathing was uneven. I sat down near her with tears in my eyes, thinking about Anita's lifeless body wrapped under those blankets. Thyme sat on the sand beside me, not saying a word.

Suddenly footsteps sounded across the sand and Patrick came running towards Olivia. He paused when he saw her. "Olivia," he said, his voice just loud enough to hear over the waves, but low enough to keep calm. "They are all looking for you. I knew you'd be here."

"Do you remember our honeymoon?" Olivia asked, her voice thin and strained. "I'd been in love with the ocean. I've always loved the ocean. But I could barely swim enough to hold myself above water. I used to dream about it every night. We came here on our honeymoon." There were tears in her voice and I could see the blood on her arm in the moon light.

"Yes," Patrick agreed, sounding slightly on edge. "The deserted beach was your favorite part." His voice was careful, as if talking to a wounded animal. "Love, why don't you step away from the water, let me take a look at that arm."

"I can't swim," Olivia repeated. "And that used to stand between me and the ocean. But not anymore. Not tonight. I've realized, why let it keep me away?" her voice lowered. "Why let that be a problem?"

"Darling, you can't swim. It's not safe. Please step back from the water."

Although it seemed it, her next act was nothing of defiance but of desperation and she stepped forward and let the water rush up to her knees.

"Olivia!" Patrick shouted, sounding worried. "I need to tell you something."

"Tell me," Olivia said and her hands rested flat against the water. Her body automatically shivered from the temperature of it, but she didn't move away.

Patrick took careful steps towards the water, pulling his shoes from his feet before stepping into it as well. He gasped and nearly backed out of the icy water, but he continued forward, forcing himself towards what was more important.

"There is a disease," he started. "Called Manic-Depressive Psychosis. Have you heard of it?"

Olivia waited a long time before she answered. A heavy wave came up and lifted her, slowly settling her deeper in the water. It was now up to her waist. Patrick's movements were less graceful. He was wading through the water quickly, splashing it everywhere. His body shook uncontrollably. "No," Olivia finally said. "No I haven't."

Patrick continued forward. "Well I'll tell you about it," he said. "It is a mental disorder. It's like a sickness of the brain. But it can be cured through therapy and medicine. It causes your emotions to spin out of line. You can suddenly become too angry or too happy or sad. You have no control over it. It can make you do dreadful things without your realization, until it's too late."

"Why are you telling me about this?" Olivia's tone was

flat and curious all at once.

I followed after Patrick, wanting to get closer. Since the water went right through me, I moved quickly along, unlike Patrick who kept tripping and forcing his way forwards.

"Because I think I may have it," he admitted, and Olivia didn't respond. He was finally getting closer to her. "And I'd like to get help." A wave hit him in the back, hard, and he stumbled forward, reaching Olivia. "I've hurt you. I never meant to but I did."

He slowly traced the cut on Olivia's arm and she flinched. The salt in the wound seemed to wake her up a bit and she finally turned to Patrick. Silent tears were running down her face.

"Anita is dead," she whispered and Patrick wrapped his arms around her, pulling her tightly to him.

"I know," he cried quietly. "I'm sorry."

Olivia closed her eyes and the water that was moving around them suddenly lifted higher, creating a huge wave that slammed into the both of them. They lost their grip and were thrown into the water, far away from shore. Patrick brought himself up for air after a moment, gasping it in and turning in circles. He coughed and spit water and turned in circles around and around. "Olivia!" he shouted, fear overtaking him when he found the water empty.

I blinked and I was back on the shore, watching everything from far away. Suddenly, I couldn't breathe. I started to cough but my lungs just continued to close in on me.

"Olivia!" the voice shouted again.

The sand around me blurred to water. I felt the cold water pushing me further under. The salt burned my eyes and my lungs and the wound on my arm. I moved my arms frantically, only being pulled further under. And then I let go and let it take me, feeling the calm ocean save me from my grief.

Even when hands took my arms and pulled me up, I didn't breathe.

When someone shouted my name, breathed into my lungs, and pounded on my chest, I didn't return.

It took me forever to even realize that I was no longer in the water. My entire body was numb and it felt nice.

I was trapped in this body and I was watching all at once. The last thing that occurred to me was big blue eyes that cried and begged and watched me as if I was the most precious thing in the world.

Part Two
Alexandra

I felt the features of my body shifting and I gasped for air, though I no longer needed it. My pale skin turned a beautiful olive tone. My hair grew shorter, my face rounder, my body more petite and curvier. The hair that just fell below my shoulders shifted and I leaned forward and saw it was nearly black.

I took in my surroundings, expecting to see the white blank world again, and found myself in a small, blurry room. "Hello Jane Doe," Thyme said, walking up to me. She was slightly shadowy. "Is this my second life?" I guessed, beginning to understand.

She placed something over my eyes and my vision cleared. They must have been glasses.

"Sorry, but Alexandra's vision isn't the best. Don't worry though, she tends to wear contacts."

"She *did*," I croaked and realized that my voice was different, foreign yet familiar to my ears. "That's how Olivia dies?"

"Yes," Thyme said.

"But why did I go through it too?"

"Because the clearest memory of death is what it feels like," Thyme explained.

"How would you know? You've never died. You are just an angel," I said in my new, naturally hoarse voice.

Thyme frowned. "I'm no angel," she said, and avoided the question, going on to point out the crib beside me. "You just witnessed Olivia's end. But press play for Alex's beginning."

I nodded slowly. "Can I ask you a question first?" I started, and she sighed.

"Yes Jane Doe?"

"If you are not an angel then... what are you?"

Thyme stared for a long moment, not really wanting to answer. "It's not what I am," she said slowly. "It's what I was."

"Which is... what exactly?" I pushed, really wanting to understand more.

Thyme disappeared without giving an answer.

I stood there for a long time, but then I gave up, turning towards the crib, and whispering, "Play."

A baby in the crib stirred and began to cry, stretching her small, pudgy hands in the air. There was a dark patch of hair on her head. Her nose was small and her lips were full. She had a single tooth just peeking through her gums. She screamed louder and a woman ran into the room, taking the small child into her arms. She looked just like the child: dark black hair, small nose, brown eyes- it had to be her mother.

The way she cradled the baby, holding her close, making her feel safe... it was all familiar. "Anita," I whispered, and I smile widely. "Mom."

She was reincarnated into my mother. This time she was mine and I would always be hers. "Shh. Alexandra, it's okay," she cooed to the baby, her accent clearly American. The baby continued to cry and her mother held her and rocked her, and soon the baby was drifting back to sleep in her arms. The woman carried her downstairs and into a very modern looking kitchen. There was a marble island and a wooden table and a white, old-looking fridge. A man walked into the room and, before I could assume he was her husband, the woman called him 'Daddy' and asked where he had been.

"Grocery store," he said, taking off his coat and hanging it over the chair. His belly was thick and his hair was grey.

He proceeded to lift a paper grocery bag and began to

unload it. "Guess she's not sleeping through the night yet, huh *Pami*?" the man asked.

The woman didn't bother answering. She fluffed her hair and it looked like a style from the eighties. The phone rang and she placed young Alexandra into her grandfather's arms, where she stirred slightly. He looked down at his granddaughter, smiling.

"You know," he said as soon as she got off the phone. "Rich would be really proud of your little girl. I'm sorry he never got to meet her."

Pam stared for a long time and then took Alexandra from her father. "I'm gonna put her back in bed," she said, her voice betraying how she was really feeling.

I closed my eyes, wanting to see more of this young girl. If Anita/Pam was my mother, then life must have been okay. But who was Rich? And where was he?

Meeting

"Alex," Pam said and the dizziness in this life was not nearly as bad as the last. "Alex, I would like you to meet somebody."

I turned slightly to see that I was standing in the middle of a backyard decorated with picnic benches, a tent, ribbons, food, party games, balloons, etc. There was a young girl next to Pam with the same big brown eyes and dark hair as the baby. She was clearly Alex. She had to have been five or six. Her hair was cut to her shoulders.

Alex hid shyly behind Pamela and behind the woman across from her I could see two feet on the ground. Both women laughed out loud. "On the count of three Maggie?" Pam asked and Maggie nodded.

"One," Pam said. "Two," Maggie went on. And then they both said, "Three!"

At the same time, they spun around, grabbed a small child, and held them up in the air. Both children were giggling loudly. "Devin, this is Alex. Alex this is Devin," Maggie introduced. "Now you both have somebody to talk to."

While Alex wore a black dress, Devin wore a checkered button up shirt and jeans with elastic at the waist. He had a bowl haircut. "You have a boy's name!" Devin accused and his mom reprimanded him.

"It's short for *Alexandra*," Alex defended and the mothers looked worried. "And anyway, your haircut is stupid!"

"Is not!" Devin shouted back and scowled.

"Is too!"

"Alex!" Pam gasped. "That's not nice! Look you two, we know that neither of you want to be here. But can you at least *try* to be friends?"

Alex and Devin stared for a long time and then Alex

muttered, "Fine. Let's go play on the swing set."

The two turned and walked away. "I don't like swing sets," Devin said and Alex pushed him.

Thyme didn't usually scare me anymore, but when she appeared right in front of me, I gasped. "Those two are so *cute*! It's like love at first sight," she beamed.

I forced myself up. "Where were you?" I demanded.

"Watching another life. Look, no more personal questions."

"But…"

"If you want me to stay then no more, okay?

"Okay," I huffed and stood up.

"Look. You already have Alex's attitude!" Thyme cooed and laughed as Alex pushed Devin on the swings, so hard that he actually fell off.

I couldn't help but laugh too.

Sunset

"Shh," a child whispered.

It was Devin and beside him was Alex. They were only a year or two older since they first met. The two of them lay in the grass, staring up at the sunset above them in a small backyard. "Devin," Alex said. "Why—"

He shushed her again. "This one. It's another one of those sunsets."

"Mercy's Sunset?" Alex smiled widely.

Their hands clasped tightly between them, they watched in wonder as the sun sunk below the trees and the sky broke out into orange, pink, yellow, purple.

I tilted my head back, taking in the beautiful sky above me, the world around me. I could practically feel the life I'd left behind. It was so close. But then it was dark and Alex's mom was calling the children in for dinner.

Fight

I was standing in the middle of a hallway to a place that brought me nothing but dread. As I blinked away the slight nausea, I saw kids piling through the hallways, exiting classrooms, opening lockers… it was so awful that I nearly blinked myself right out of it. But I didn't when I saw a shorter girl with dark brown hair, glasses, red lipstick, big brown eyes, a black shirt, and black jeans. Oh, and a small red streak in the front of her hair.

Walking through the hallway, she bumped into a tall skinny blond girl who didn't even look at her as she continued through the hallway. "Jesus!" Alex hissed.

Just by looking at her, I could tell that she was fifteen or sixteen. "Devin!" Alex suddenly called in a raspy voice and stomped forwards. A tall, older version of Devin turned around. The second he saw her, Devin spun and tried to run down the hallway. "Oh no you don't! Get back here Devin Malky!"

She dropped her bag in the middle of the hallway and began to run at him, cutting through the crowds of people and literally jumping onto his back to stop him. Devin gasped and tripped into a classroom, catching his balance. He no longer looked like a nerd. He wore baggy jeans and a t-shirt that said *Guns N' Roses*. "What did I do?" she demanded, clinging to his back tightly.

"Get off!" Devin begged. "Damn it! You weigh a ton!"

"I do *not*! And tell me what I did to make you so angry!"

Alex's hair was a mess in her face and her long bangs covered her eyes.

"No!" Devin insisted.

Alex wrapped her knees around his hips and locked her elbow around his neck. Devin growled under his breath and he tried to get air in. Alex lowered her mouth next to his ear and her voice was low when she spoke again. "Tell me," she hissed quietly and Devin finally gave in, his face turning purple.

I couldn't help but smile when he croaked, "You told my mom I got a D on the last history quiz."

Alex's eyes widened and she smirked, releasing his neck and dropping to her feet gracefully, like a cat with nine lives. She snorted a laugh and Devin narrowed his eyes. "What's so funny?" he demanded.

"I-I never did that," Alex laughed. "You left the quiz in the middle of the kitchen table. When you went to get something from your room, and your mom was giving me one of her homemade cookies, she saw it and asked me very nicely to leave so she could, *please speak to her son.*"

Alex smirked and brushed her hair out of her face. That's when I noticed the small nose ring she had. She readjusted her t-shirt so it hung over her shoulder slightly, revealing her tanned skin. Devin just stood there for a long moment and finally said, "So you never told her?"

Alex rolled her eyes and snorted again. I vaguely wondered if that affected her nose ring. "Can't help it if you are stupid Dev. You do that all on your own."

Devin looked down sheepishly. "Well then. I guess I owe you an apology." A teacher with receding white hair clumsily entered the classroom and he nodded at Devin. "Mr. Fench," Devin mumbled and grabbed Alex by her elbow, pulling her from the room.

"You sure do owe me an apology," she shot back, entering the busy hallway. "You can't shut me out like that sweetie. I'm your *best friend*. Melanie wasn't at school today. So who did I have left? I had to eat with that girl Janie. You know, the one with the braces, headgear stuff? All she eats is applesauce and Jell-O, and she even manages to get that caught in her metal teeth."

Devin nodded slowly and linked arms with Alex. She was much shorter than him and struggled to reach his height. She was barely 5'2 and Devin must have been over six feet. "Alright, alright," Devin gave in. "Look, I can't go to the movies with you this weekend."

"Why? You got a date with Mandy?" Alex teased, but there was an edge to her voice.

"No," Devin assured. "I'm *grounded* thanks to my wonderful history talents." He stopped to open a locker, easily spinning the code and pulling out a bag before tossing it over his shoulder.

He then eyed Alex's bag which still resided in the middle of the hallway. It had been stepped on and slightly trampled, and her books had fallen out of the open zipper. Devin raised an eyebrow and then moved to begin piling the books back into the bag. Alex crossed her arms and waited until the bag was filled to take it. "*Gracias*," she sang in an almost perfect Spanish accent.

I giggled, finding her very amusing. She linked arms with Devin again and practically dragged him from the school, down the steps, and across the front lawn where jocks tossed a football back and forth. One throw nearly caused the ball to hit Alex in the face, but Devin released her arm and caught it, re-aiming and throwing it back to a big guy with more fat than muscle. "Watch it Brady," Devin warned.

"Ass-hole!" Alex shrieked, giving the finger, and Devin pulled her along before she could lose her cool. "I hate those damn losers. How can you hang out with them?"

Devin shrugged, looking uncomfortable. "I can have more than one friend Alex," he reminded her.

Alex smirked maniacally. "That's what you think," she said, her voice highly sarcastic and Devin chuckled. "But seriously Dev, they are *bullies* and you are too good for them."

"Thanks," Devin sighed.

"Anyways," Alex went on. "Since you are grounded and can't see a movie, I guess I'll have to find a way to sneak in. What movie should I bring?"

"No, no," Devin sighed. "I'm already in enough trouble Al. Just make plans with Melanie."

"Mel has plans with *Brian*. Haven't you figured out by now that he is supposed to come first? He's her boyfriend. I gave her permission."

"That's very kind of you," Devin chuckled and pulled his arm free to remove a pack of cigarettes from his pocket.

He pulled one out and stopped to place it in his mouth, retrieving a lighter from his pocket and cupping one hand around the cigarette as he used his other hand to light it. "You should really quit," Alex told him. "Smoking is so bad for you."

"Oh please," Devin chuckled. "Everyone does it."

Alex rolled her eyes and plucked the cigarette from his mouth. "Hey," Devin gasped as she placed it in her own mouth and inhaled deeply.

Seconds later, Alex was coughing up a storm and Devin took the cigarette back, balancing it in his own mouth as he waited for Alex to catch her breath, and her eyes filled with tears. "How the hell do you like that?" she spluttered between coughs.

"It gets better," Devin said. "But you are totally killing my buzz."

He dropped the cigarette to the ground and stepped on it while Alex pulled out a bottle of water and practically gulped it down. Smoke was still flowing out of her nostrils and Devin easily blew a thin trail of smoke out. I made a face at it. Thinking of smoking repulsed me even now and I smelled the smoke as it drifted towards me. Still, just like when Mr. Minster had smoked around Olivia, the smoke didn't burn my lungs. It just smelled bad.

The duo stopped in front of an old, run down, brick house. "Here we are," Alex said, her voice slightly hoarse from the coughing.

There was a small smudge of the thick eyeliner under Alex's eye from the way the smoke caused her eyes to tear. Devin told her to hold still as he reached his thumb forwards to carefully wipe the eyeliner. Alex's breath caught in her throat as his hand made contact with her skin. When he moved his hand away, he quickly broke the eye contact that the two had been holding just a moment ago.

"You, uh, do you wanna come inside?" Alex offered, her voice small and careful.

Devin hesitated and then shook his head. "I would love to Al, but I'm grounded. Remember?"

"Right," Alex muttered. "You gotta stop getting your stupid ass in trouble."

She reached out her hand and they did this odd handshake where they shook, slapped the back of their hands together and then the front before they quickly pulled them away. "See ya Dev. Give me a call. I'll be nice and bored considerin' I already got my homework done."

"Dork," Devin said, but I knew he was joking. "I'll try and make time for you, Doll."

Alex stuck out her tongue. Devin turned and left. "Jerk!" she called, giggling.

Daddy

The room was small and the walls were painted red. It was dark outside through the shaded window in the room and there were a few pieces of furniture, but nothing like Olivia's rich house.

Alex lay back on her bed with her eyes closed. Her hair was a wet mess around her head and she wore pajamas. It was only a few hours later. I barely felt the discomfort in my head.

Alex's eyes opened and she looked over at a picture next to her bed of a man with thick, dark hair, and Pamela when she was younger, pregnant with Alex probably. Without makeup, Alex looked much younger, and I started to debate how old she really was.

There was a knock at the door and it opened without any answer. Pam walked in and sat on the side of Alex's bed. "Grandpa called," she told her. "He's worried. He hasn't heard from you this week."

"I called him on Saturday. It's *Tuesday*." Alex rolled her eyes. "I'm fine Mom."

"Mhm," Pamela hummed knowingly and then motioned for Alex to scoot over. Alex moved over and Pam lay down next to her. "Now," Pam said. "Tell me what's really up."

Alex closed her eyes, but she didn't answer. She played with her nose ring. I noticed, now that her hair had fallen back, that her right cartilage was pierced as well with a small gold hoop in it. "Devin was a little mad at me today," she finally admitted.

"How come?" Pam asked, sounding concerned.

"It's stupid," Alex muttered. "He blamed me for something I didn't do. We made up and that's it."

"But?" Pam prodded.

"But..." Alex sighed deeply. "For those few hours without him, and Melanie was home by the way, I felt...

very lonely. I don't have a whole lot of friends." She picked at the black nail polish on her fingernails. "And *Man-Made-Mandy* was *all over* him. I just had to sit there and watch."

Pam stared for a while. "Number one, why do you call her... whatever it is that you call her? And number two, why does it bother you so much that she may like Devin? You aren't dating him."

Alex looked down at her hands and bit her lip. "She has bleach-blond hair that is cut really short- like so short that she would look like a man if it weren't for those huge fake *boobs* that she has. I mean, those *can't* be real." Alex looked down at her own chest and frowned. "Her nose is clearly fake too. And her fingernails. And I bet her ass--"

"Okay," Pam cut Alex off. "That is none of your business and you know it. Now answer my second question."

Alex shrugged her shoulders, her eyes narrowing. "I love Devin. He's my best friend ever. I can't lose him to that fake Mandy with her *fake* hair and her *fake* nails and her *fake-*"

"Okay," Pamela stopped her once again. "Stop talking about fake things. It's not like your hair naturally has that red streak."

Alex rolled her eyes and looked over at Pam for a long moment and then finally she said "How did you know you loved Dad?" and her voice shook as she said it.

This question seemed to take Pam by surprise. At first she didn't quite know what to say. And then finally she looked honestly at Alex. "Ally," she said. "I was waiting on your father back when I used to work at that diner in college. He was so sweet to me. He spoke to me like a human being and not like the girl who he was paying to get him food. He even asked me to sit with him and talk for a while. I didn't know I loved him then. He started coming by every day. He would stay long after he finished his coffee. Then one day, he admitted to me that he didn't even like coffee. He was there for another reason. He finally worked up the courage to ask me out on a real date.

"By then, it already felt like we had been dating forever. After a few months he asked me to marry him. Of course I said yes. A year later, we got a house instead of an apartment. A year after that, I got pregnant with you. Three months after that, a drunk driver killed him in an accident, as you well know. And he never got to meet you." Pam's voice was strained. "So there you have it. I loved him very much. I knew it when we were together. I knew it even more when he was gone and I couldn't tell it to him anymore."

Alex was looking at Pam with tears in her eyes and hugged her tightly. The phone began to ring. Both of them pulled away and Pam quickly stood, forcing a tight smile at Alex, and then left the room. Alex cleared her throat and blinked a few times before picking up the phone. I turned up the volume.

"Hey Al," Devin said on the other line.

"Well it's about time you called," Alex responded and a smile appeared on her full lips.

Hangout

As the world shifted, I felt a slight dizziness that quickly wore off. A girl with golden hair sat next to Alex, who was lying upside down on the bed. She looked a little older. She was not wearing any makeup and she was still in her pajamas. Her red streak was gone and replaced with a blue one. Based on the sun outside, it was early in the morning. "You really won't come to school?" Blondie asked. "You look *fine*."

"Do not," Alex mumbled and when she turned her face, I saw a huge bandage across her forehead.

"Where do you keep disappearing to?" I demanded when I felt the light breeze from behind me.

"Don't worry about it," Thyme replied and stared at Alex from next to me.

Thyme's usually life-filled eyes were now careful and sad. I didn't even ask, afraid that she would abandon me again. The truth was that having her around was better than watching this all by myself. "What's wrong with you?" I asked.

"Same answer," Thyme muttered and I looked back at Alex who was staring at the girl with gold hair.

"I am so effin' clumsy," Alex hissed and Blondie laughed.

"Yes you are," she agreed.

"Come on Mel," Alex insisted. "Just go to school."

I realized that the girl was Melanie, Alex's other good friend. She was much skinnier than Alex and she was naturally beautiful, wearing only a bit of light brown eye shadow.

The door opened and Thyme stepped aside, as if to let Devin pass her, even though he could walk right through her.

"Your mom says you're not talking to anyone," Devin said, walking into Alex's room.

"I'm talking to Mel," Alex said.

"Barely," Melanie murmured. "Devin, could you take care of Mope-y over here? She's giving me a migraine."

"Go find your boyfriend," Devin chuckled, and I knew immediately that these two weren't very good friends, but they were civil.

As soon as Melanie left and shut the door, Devin climbed up onto the full-sized bed with her and lay upside down as well, staring up at the ceiling fan like Alex did. Thyme whistled to make fun of them being in bed together, but I ignored her.

"So Al, you decided to trip over a rock and hit your head on a brick wall? Did you really think that was such a great idea?"

Alex shoved him in the side. "You shut up! It's not like I did it on purpose!"

"Are you in pain?" Devin asked simply.

"No," Alex grumbled.

"So why won't you come to school?"

"Because I look like shit!"

"Ooh, language," Devin teased and ran his finger down the side of Alex's face. "And yes Ally, you do look like shit."

Alex narrowed her eyes, but I could tell that she was too focused on Devin's finger that still lightly traced the bandage on her forehead. Then, without warning, Devin pulled his hand away, wrapped his arm around her shoulders from underneath her, and pulled her close. Alex rested her head on his chest. "I'm not going to school," she said stubbornly, tracing her finger along Devin's chest as if it was completely natural to do.

Devin's eyes had fixated on her fingers and he slowly drew them away to stare at her face. "Huh? Oh, well, if you're not going, neither am I."

Alex rolled her eyes. "Go to school Devin," she told him, brushing her fingers through her bangs so they would cover her forehead.

"Nope. If you're staying, then I'm staying."

"You don't have to do that."

"I'm your best friend. It's my job." Alex wiggled her toes and Devin stared down at her bare feet. "Your feet cold?" he asked and when Alex nodded her head, he moves his legs over her feet to warm them up.

"Can they just admit they like each other already?" Thyme teased and I motioned for her to shut up.

Devin rested his head on top of Alex's. "What do I have to do to get you to go to school?"

Alex seemed to think this over for a long time. "Um... break up with Mandy."

Devin frowned and I gaped. "He's dating *her*?" I shrieked, and Thyme eyed me with a smirk on her face.

"No," Devin muttered. "Seriously though."

"Fine," Alex said and she seemed to consider just what she wanted. "You eat with *me* today and *not* Mandy."

"Alex," Devin started to warn but she grasped his shirt with her hand.

"Please?" she begged and he finally gave in.

"You have two minutes to get dressed and get ready for school."

Alex sighed and stood up, running around her room to grab clothes from her closet and her black eyeliner and red lipstick. "Four minutes," she told Devin and disappeared from the room before he could object.

Party

"You look lovely," Pamela said as Alex descended the stairs, wearing a sleeveless, sparkling, silver dress.

Her hair was tied back behind her head and she wore a black hat and a black blazer. "Lovely?" Alex's grandfather said, eyeing Pam wearily. "She looks like a tramp."

"*She* is right here Grandpa," Alex laughed lightly and gave him a hug before kissing her mom on the cheek.

"Be back by midnight," Pam said.

"Midnight?" her grandfather demanded. "Do you know how many guys can—"

"Dad!" Pam stopped him and then winked at Alex. "Have a good time baby."

"Love you Mom," Alex said and left the house to where Melanie was waiting in her car.

Her golden hair was now cropped to her shoulders and her makeup was very overdone. Still, she looked beautiful. "Woo, Alex!" she cheered as Alex got into the car. "Showing off some cleavage tonight? Competing with Devin's girl?"

"Mandy's are fake. These are perfectly real," Alex assured her, and giggled.

The sun was still out and the sky was turning shades of blue and purple.

"I really like her dress," Thyme said as we walked through the car door and took a seat in the back.

"I don't think Alex likes it very much," I told her. "Because I can't stand it."

"She's probably wearing it to make Devin jealous," Thyme said, and my stomach twisted.

"I have a really bad feeling," I admitted. Thyme didn't respond, but I knew she heard me.

"Why don't you just tell Devin you like him?" Melanie asked as they begin to drive.

Alex rolled her eyes in response and I found myself doing the same thing. But I couldn't shake the bad feeling. "Because I *don't!*" Alex hissed.

"Oh you do," Melanie responded and Alex huffed a sigh.

"He's just a friend."

"No. I'm just a friend. He's so much more than that. He settled for Man-Made-Mandy. If you told him you liked him already, he would be all over you before the night is over."

"That's enough Mel," Alex sighed and looked out the window. "You really think he likes me?"

Mel smirked to herself. "Yes," she said. "He loves you."

"I wouldn't say that he loves me," Alex said, her cheeks turning bright red. "So what should I do?"

"Tell him!"

"But that would ruin everything if he doesn't like me back and we both know it."

Slowly, I looked out the window as we came to a stoplight. I just stared for a moment until I saw a car next to ours. There was a girl with cropped, bleach-blond hair and lots of face rings. She was very skinny, yet her chest was too huge to be real. Devin sat next to her and as he stopped the car, he quickly leaned in to kiss her before he turned back to driving. Anger bubbled inside of me and I looked up front to see Alex staring, doing the same thing. "You see?" Alex said and Mel's expression showed she did. "He likes *her*. Let's just keep things the way they are. Okay?"

Melanie said nothing as she continued to drive once the light turned green. I looked over at Devin again and he was staring straight ahead of him, periodically glancing back at Melanie's car. He had seen Alex as well.

I blinked and flashed to the party. Already, people were crowded around the front lawn. Alex stepped out of the car.

Her watch said that it is just past seven. The sun was drooping lower in the sky. Devin pulled up his fancy sports car and parked, saying something to Mandy. She snapped back at him and he rolled his eyes before saying something else and getting out of the car. I was too angry to turn up the volume to hear what they were saying. Mandy's skirt was short and her top cut down low, showing off her big, fake boobs. "I bet if Alex punched her in the chest, she wouldn't feel it." I smirked. "Those things *can't* be real."

"Stop looking," Thyme admonished.

Devin quickly made his way over to Alex, grabbing her arm. "Hey," he said.

Alex yanked her arm free. "Hey," she grumbled back.

"You remember when we were young, and I used to say that certain sunsets would be so beautiful you would almost feel merciful?" Alex didn't look at him but she frowned, nodding slowly. "It looks like that now," Devin said.

Alex glanced at the sky. Clouds covered the setting sun and they shined with pink, blue, orange, red, and purple. "Yeah," Alex whispered, looking in the distance. "Pretty."

She turned and walked away. Devin was quick to follow after. "Alex, what do you want from me?"

"I don't know what you mean!" she lied.

"Why don't you just talk to me?"

"There's nothing to talk about," Alex said, her eyes hard. "I need a drink."

"You don't drink," Devin reminded her.

"Well tonight I'll try one."

"Yeah you do that."

Devin pulled out a cigarette and rested it in his mouth as he began to light it. Alex made a sound of disgust and began to walk away. "What?" Devin called.

"Put out the damn *effin'* cigarette!" Alex yelled and Devin inhaled sharply and exhaled the smoke through his nose.

71

"No," he told her simply.

She growled and stomped her foot angrily. "Screw you!"

"Jesus Alex, could you stop acting like a child? Just grow the hell up," Devin snapped and Alex turned to him with tears in her eyes.

"Don't talk to me," she said, pointing a finger at him. "Leave me the hell alone!"

Devin grasped her arm hard and swung her around to look at him. He spit out his cigarette and stomped on it, smashing out the flames with his foot. "I didn't do anything wrong."

"Of course not," Alex muttered and tried to pull her arm free but Devin pulled her behind the house and released her, crossing his arms over his chest.

"Talk to me," he pleaded.

Alex narrowed her eyes and for a moment, I nearly thought she was going to say *it*- the exact words that Mel had told her to say. But instead she just stepped back and whispered, "Devin, I have nothing to say to you right now."

She tried to blink her tears away as she turned to leave. She collided with Mandy on the way in and they glared at each other as she left, stepping in the exact spot where Devin left his cigarette.

"She's an idiot," Thyme said.

"Gee thanks. You do realize that she is me, right?" I pointed out.

"Yep," Thyme said simply, and I sighed.

"She *is* an idiot," I agreed quietly, and followed Alex into the house.

The house was dark and Christmas lights illuminated the house in gold. One room held kids smoking. Another room held kids drinking. The living room held Melanie and the guy who I assumed was her boyfriend, Brian. She took a sip of her drink from a red cup and Alex snatched it from her hand. Mel frowned. "That bad?" she asked over the loud, blasting music, and Alex didn't answer.

Instead, she took a long sip of the drink, scrunched up her nose in disgust, and forced the drink down. For a moment she placed the cup back into Melanie's hand and she gagged. But then she relaxed and took the drink back. She chugged it down, all of it, and staggered a bit. "Whoa, slow down," Brian chuckled and Alex ignored him, taking his drink next.

Alex drank that one, leaving the room. She got a refill and I could feel the room growing blurry and my head spinning. "What's going on?" I slurred out.

"This memory is from when you were drunk," Thyme explained.

"Don't I control this?" I asked, hating the sick feeling.

I gagged, but I didn't throw up. I couldn't.

"You don't control what the memories are. You just control what you're watching."

I closed my eyes and fast forwarded the night, but the haziness only got worse. I tipped onto the ground, feeling my head spin and my memory blur and my stomach heave.

I tried to fast forward more, practically losing my ability to. Finally, I found that the room stopped spinning and Alex was dancing with some guy that I had never seen before. She was sweating like crazy and her hair stuck to the back of her neck. Her hat was nowhere in sight, and neither was her jacket.

Glancing at the clock, I saw that it is already ten o'clock and Alex had made no progress with Devin. The guy she was dancing with whispered something to her and I couldn't quite find the energy to turn up the volume. Alex muttered a no. The guy gave her arm a tug and insisted. Alex seemed to sober up a bit and the blurry world grew clearer. She slurred out another no, and the guy began to grow agitated. He pulled her harder and she tried to scream.

Devin suddenly stepped through the crowd and pushed the boy aside. He became angry, but he was too drunk to fight back. Devin was as sober as they came. "Come on," he said to Alex.

He was holding her hat and blazer in his hand. Alex shook her head but he lifted her up and tossed her over his shoulder. She protested and slammed her fists against his back and mumbled objections as he carried her outside.

My vision was growing slightly clearer, and I knew that Alex was sobering up. I felt a billion times better.

Devin carried her to his car. "So what? Are you gonna take me home now? Are you going to act like my parent? Force me to listen to you? And where's Man-Made-Mandy? Shouldn't you be taking her home? I mean, she's seen you so much more than I have lately. You don't fight with her. Only with me."

"She is really intoxicated," Thyme sighed, shaking her head.

"I do fight with her," Devin admitted, his voice on the edge of bitterness. "That's why we just broke up. Because I told her that I wouldn't stop being your friend. Are you happy now?"

This seemed to stop Alex and Devin opened the back of his car, but before he could get Alex inside, she began to thrash until he put her down and she leaned over and threw up in the grass. More of the haziness cleared away and I could see the regret in Alex's eyes as she caught her breath. Devin waited patiently, handing her a napkin. She wiped her mouth. "You broke up with her? Really?" she whispered, and opened the front door to the car, getting in.

"Really," Devin sighed and walked around the other side of the car.

"What about Melanie?" Alex asked as Thyme and I got into the back seat. I still couldn't shake the odd feeling inside of me.

"I told her I was taking you home," Devin explained.

Devin buckled himself into the car and turned his lights on. "I'm sorry," Alex suddenly whispered and Devin reached over to take her hand for a moment.

"I know," he said and squeezed her hand before he let go, starting the car.

They drove in silence for a while until Alex finally spoke.

"I just got so angry," she explained. "When I saw you kiss her... I don't know why... it just... it bothered me."

Devin's knuckles were turning white from grasping the steering wheel so hard. His focus seemed to be elsewhere and he pulled the car over on the side of the road, shutting off the engine and turning to look at Alex. "I know."

"Have you ever wondered...?" Alex started and then trailed off.

"What we'd be like if we were a couple?" Devin asked and Alex didn't say anything. Devin seemed nervous as he went on. "Yes," he admitted. "You've been my best friend for years. Every time we would stare at Mercy's Sunset together, I used to wonder... what it would be like if I just leaned over and... kissed you."

Alex nodded slowly. A light rain began to hit the top of the car and in the dark I could hear Alex breathing heavily. She looked like she was about to talk but Devin stopped her.

"Just let me talk, okay? I need to say this out loud. Mandy liked me. Everyone would tell me to go for it. And I did. But I often wondered... what was it I saw in her? I wanted something real. And with you... I think I might be able to have that. But I never know what would happen to us as friends. I'm just... so terrified of losing that."

"But?" Alex prodded and Devin just shook his head, not going on like she wanted him to.

The bad feeling hit me harder. I wanted to warn them

but I couldn't and I didn't even know what I wanted to warn them about. Thyme told me to relax and based on the look in her eyes, she knew exactly what was going on.

"There is no 'but'," Alex concluded, and Devin said nothing. "You don't like me like that, so that's it, right?"

"Alex," Devin sighed.

"Devin, just don't."

Devin unbuckled his seatbelt and turned to touch the side of Alex's face. "I do... like you like that. I do." Alex stopped breathing and I did too (not that I even needed to breathe in the first place, but still.) If my heart could beat, it would be throbbing in my chest. "I just... I don't know if I'm ready. But I believe that we could be so much and—"

"I love you," Alex cut him off, having had enough of whatever he was trying to figure out. "I freaking love you Devin."

Before Devin responded, she leaned in and kissed him. The rain was now pounding on the roof of the car and it blurred out the windshield. After a moment, Devin kissed her back and ran his fingers through her hair, pulling her closer. His hand move down to her hips and she reached, about to unbuckle her seatbelt.

"No!" I suddenly shrieked.

Bam!

The car rolled and crashed and glass broke and metal bent and tires squeaked and horns honked and rain fell heavily. And then I was lying in the middle of the road, looking up at the sky, slowly waking up. Alex had blacked out for a moment, so my memory was as good as hers. Lights flickered in my blurred vision and there was loud shouting. The car had rolled and I went right through the wall of it since it couldn't quite hold me.

I saw a shape on the side of the road and I felt my ribs aching. Alex must have gotten hurt. I felt slightly connected to her at the moment as I forced myself off the ground and limped forwards.

Arms suddenly wrapped around me and held me down. "Stay," Thyme insisted, sounding worried.

"I get it," I hissed. "I'm dying. Some idiot swerved off the road and hit us. Let me see Alex now."

When she didn't answer, I understood.

Alex wasn't dying.

Then I saw the car on the side of the road. It was smashed to a shape I couldn't even understand. Alex was crawling out of the car. She forced herself to her shaky feet and limped through the rain. "Devin," she croaked out and I screamed louder for Thyme to let me go. "Devin!"

I sent my elbow backwards, knocking Thyme straight off of me, and I forced myself forwards.

The man in the other car screamed for help, stopping a car that was passing by. I finally caught up to Alex and watched as she looked all around her. There were blood stains on the windshield of the car. Devin's seat was empty.

"Devin!" Alex repeated, her voice incredibly weak.

Finally, she saw something, and I saw it at the same time. There was a figure up ahead. Its body was mangled, lying at an odd angle. It twitched slightly. It was so messed up and covered in blood that, at first, I almost didn't even realize that it was Devin. When I did, I blinked and I was next to him.

I fell to my knees on the road. Alex screamed in a hoarse voice as she made her way over to him. "Stay with me!" she cried and screamed for help.

Devin's eyes were barely open. He kept mumbling the same thing again and again. I couldn't make out what he was saying. The rain was pounding overhead. "Devin!" Alex begged. "Can you hear me? Devin!"

Devin looked up at her and his eyes tried to fix on her in the darkness. He whispered "Ally" and his eyes closed and he fell still.

Lights were flashing all around us. Alex's face went blank and she gently sunk to the ground next to him as I just watched. She closed her eyes and rested her head on Devin's unmoving chest.

Her eyes suddenly flashed open and she coughed heavily against her hand. When she pulled it back, it was covered in blood. She showed no emotion. She simply lay her head back against his chest. Seconds later, her eyes rolled back into her head and I felt hazy as the world went blank.

Knowing

A man stared at me. He was familiar and handsome and as he whispered, "Alexandra" I felt as if I'd known him forever. His smile comforted me until he vanished.

As my vision cleared, I could hear beeping and the room was small and white with florescent lights. Alex lay in bed, scars and stitches and casts holding her together. "Ally?" a man whispered. "Alexandra?"

I looked next to her bed and I saw her mother sitting there, holding her hand and resting her head against it. Her grandfather was rising from a chair on the other side of the room and walking towards the bed. "Pam," her grandfather said, shaking her mother, who sat straight up. Her eyes were bloodshot and glassy. She groaned under her breath and I realized that that is what Alex's grandfather heard. Now Pam was wide awake and whispering Alex's name as well. Alex mumbled something under her breath and Pam pleaded with her to say it again.

"Dad-dy?" Alex got out, her voice hoarse and underused.

Tears filled Pam's eyes and she leaned over and sobbed against the hand that held onto Alex's.

"Ally?" her grandfather said once again. "Sweetheart, open your eyes please."

Alex grumbled and blinked a few times and her eyes rolled a bit as she looked around the room. Slowly, her relaxed, confused gaze grew serious and dreadful. "Grandpa?" she whispered. "Mommy?"

Both looked up at her and Pam's crying caught in her throat. "A-Alex," she stammered. "Baby can you hear me?"

"Devin?" Alex muttered and Pam's lips quivered.

"Alex," her grandfather said softly. "You were in a car accident. Do you remember that?"

"Devin?" Alex repeated.

79

"You broke some ribs. One of them punctured a lung and it collapsed. The doctors had to do some surgery. They saved your life but... healing will be a long process."

Alex blinked once and then said, "Devin," but her voice was surer as she got the words out. "Dead?"

Pam was sobbing so hard that I couldn't even recognize her anymore beneath the tears. Finally, Alex's grandfather pulled himself together and said, "Yes dear. He didn't make it. I'm sorry."

Just like Devin would say, Alex whispered "I know," and she was asleep again.

I didn't realize how hard I was crying until Thyme, who had been watching silently, took my hand. "W-why?" I stuttered. "Why didn't you tell me this would happen?"

"That's not how it works," Thyme sighed. "I'm sorry Jane Doe."

"I can't do this anymore," I wept. "No more, Thyme. Please."

Thyme's eyes were sad and she stepped away and disappeared.

After Effect

I knew a lot of time had passed because my head spun harder than usual. It must have been at least a few years. Devin was about seventeen when he died, and now Alex must be about twenty-one.

She sat in a chair in a therapist's office and stared out the window at cars that rushed by. "When was the last time you were truly happy?" a woman asked.

She was short and stout with graying brown hair and glossy eyes.

Alex's hair had grown long, down her back. Her brown eyes held nearly no life in them, and she wore glasses. "That's hard to say," Alex whispered, distracted.

"And why is that?" the woman prodded.

Alex didn't answer for a long time, but the woman just waited. "I guess," Alex finally said, "The last time I was *truly* happy would be like… five seconds before the crash."

The doctor wrote something down on a pad of paper. The glasses she wore on her nose were suspended by a beaded string that hung around her neck. Her outfit covered every inch of her skin.

"Why?" she asked.

Alex continued to stare out the window. I noticed she was much skinnier than the last time I saw her. "Because he loved me," Alex whispered and her lip quivered slightly as tears filled her eyes. "He was alive."

"I know," the doctor said. "But it's time to move on. That was a long time ago."

"I get it now," Alex said, ignoring her. "What my mom says about how she loves my dad even more now that he's gone. Now I get it. You feel the loss of the love. I'm just like her."

Alex turned her face and took a deep breath. The tears stopped and she built her wall back up.

Geoffrey

The next time my mind cleared and the dizziness ceased, I saw a much older version of Melanie dragging Alex through a backyard. Alex was wearing jeans and a long shirt, although it looked to be about mid-summer. Both girls were probably twenty five now. Mel was not wearing makeup and she still looked gorgeous. The sun was blazing up ahead and Alex's eyes hid behind sunglasses. Mel's hair was still shorter, just above her shoulders, and her sunglasses rested on her head. She wore cut-off jean shorts and a bikini top. She was incredibly skinny.

Alex's hair was pulled back into a messy ponytail. She wore no makeup. But her natural look didn't do her as much justice as it used to. She looked as if she has put many more years behind her than she actually did. Lines were beginning to form around her eyes, but they were very faint. I wanted to cry. "Is this the rest of her life?" I asked, knowing that Thyme was right behind me. "Alex just lives a sad boring life, goes with the flow, lives but doesn't process; her whole life is a blur?"

"You'll see," Thyme sighed.

"This isn't my last life is it?" I suddenly realized. "Why am I watching these? I can't be all of them in the afterlife, can I? Do I have to choose or something?" Thyme gave me a knowing look and I knew I was right. "That's it, isn't it? I have to choose."

"Yes," Thyme gave in. "That's it."

"But Thyme… can I choose right now? Can't I just choose Devin and be with him right now and end this misery?"

Thyme disappeared, probably too scared to admit the answer. I glared and followed after Melanie and Alex. They met up at a pool and Melanie ran to hug a boy sitting by it. It was not Brian, but I knew he was her boyfriend based on the way she sat down beside him and started to kiss him. His arm was wrapped around her.

Alex was sweating like crazy from her long sleeves and she slowly stripped her pants off but left her shirt on. There was a small scar on the inside of her leg and I understood. The scars. She was hiding the scars from the accident.

"Come on Alex!" Melanie yelled, taking a running leap into the pool. The man with her was already in.

Alex just shook her head. "No thanks."

"Oh come on!" Mel called, and finally Alex gave in and pulled off her shirt.

She was wearing a one piece bathing suit. There was a faded scar peeking out of the top of it and a few scars on her arms. She was clearly uncomfortable, not something I would expect her to be before Devin died.

Alex took a running leap into the water and I jumped in after her, watching as the water engulfed her and she seems to relax in it. Just like in her last life, she loved the water, but in this life she could swim.

Finally Alex resurfaced and I could see the disappointment on her face as reality set back in. "Finally," Mel laughed and pushed Alex back under the water.

She quickly jumped back up, gulping in air and giving Melanie a huge shove under the water. Mel's boyfriend backed away and chuckled quietly as the two girls began a splash fight.

"Hey Dan!" a man called, running over to the pool.

Mel's boyfriend responded to him and called for him to get in. The man jumped in and Alex turned, pausing when she saw the new man. His brown hair was shaggy and hung in his face. His eyes were a pale blue, green. His smile was kind.

"Hello," he introduced himself. "My name's Geoffrey."

"Alex."

They shook hands and Alex awkwardly crossed her arms over her chest to cover her scars. "I've never seen you with Dan and Melanie before."

"I told you about her," Melanie said. "She's my best friend."

Alex tensed and shrugged. "Well now I can meet you. You know, this water's freezing."

She began to get out of the pool and Mel glared at her. She wrapped a towel around herself and sat back on a lawn chair. Geoffrey slowly followed her out of the water and sat next to her. She barely even looked at him. She just stared ahead. "Having fun?" he asked.

"Not much Geoffrey," Alex admitted.

"You can call me Geoff you know. If you want," Geoffrey offered.

"I'll keep that in mind," Alex muttered.

"I think you need to go for a walk."

"You're very assumptive."

Geoff rolled his eyes and stood, reaching for Alex's hand. She didn't object as he pulled her to her feet and grinned.

I blinked and found myself about ten minutes later. Thyme walked with me and we followed Alex and Geoff. They were now wearing their clothes over their wet bathing suits. "If you had one wish," Geoff was saying. "What would you wish for? And you can't say world peace."

Alex was looking at him with confusion in her gaze. "I'd wish for a milkshake," she said, raising an eyebrow playfully.

"I can grant that wish," Geoff responded and pulled her away from the sidewalk and towards an old diner. "The best place to eat in all of New York."

"Now I wouldn't say that."

A woman got them a table and took their order. They

each got chocolate malt milkshakes. Geoff ordered them fries too. When the waitress brought them the food, Geoff grabbed a fry and dipped it in his milkshake. Alex looked at him with disgust and, without a word, he held the milkshake covered fry out to her. She rolled her eyes, opened her mouth, and bit the french-fry, smiling. The diner smelled greasy and sweet and I felt slightly at ease here.

"You know," Geoff said, chewing a french-fry. "You're pretty cool."

"Um thanks?" Alex said, as if it was a question.

"I mean it though." He stopped to sip his milkshake and then continued. "This is the most fun I've had in a while. You're funny and you don't really seem to care about appearances or any crap like that."

Alex shivered as the air-condition hit her damp clothes. "I don't care much about anything anymore," Alex admitted, her voice serious and uncaring.

"I can tell," Geoff said and stood, moving across the booth to sit on the bench next to Alex. "So would you care if I did this?"

He moved his arm around her and Alex didn't even react. She just leaned against him. "Nope."

"Or this?" He moved closer to her.

Alex shrugged. "No."

"Or this?" He leaned in and kissed her lips gently.

"No," she whispered when he pulled back and smiled softly.

"Well good," Geoff said. "Then I know I can do it again. What do you say we do this all again maybe… Friday night? Would you care for that?"

"I don't care much for anything," Alex threw back. "But I guess if you're there, I might as well be."

Geoff winked and it was a date.

Born

This time, my head spun and I nearly fell over as I found myself in a small apartment. Melanie was standing in an old, beaten down kitchen making herself a sandwich. She had a few extra lines on her face and her hair was just below her shoulders now. She was still skinny and beautiful, but there were now blond highlights in her hair to cover up its natural color.

Alex walked into the room. She looked completely different. She wore a hint of makeup. There were definitely a few extra lines on her face. Her hair was cut to her shoulders and she wore her glasses. But those weren't even the main differences. I was drawn to staring at her huge, bulging stomach. She was not fat. She was pregnant.

"Would you look at that?" Thyme laughed. "You have a baby."

"I do?" I gasped and it seemed to hit me. I did.

I didn't remember anything about the baby. Not the name. Nothing.

Alex positioned herself in a kitchen chair and looked uncomfortable. "Any day now," Mel giggled, "you'll have a little baby in your arms."

"Yeah," Alex sighed. "Guess so."

"Any ideas for names?"

Alex shook her head. "How did you come up with Maya's name?"

"After my grandmother; Mandarin. What an odd name though, you know? I named her after Granny Mandarin and got the most adorable little Maya with the biggest brown eyes."

"She's three effin' years old." Alex shook her head.

"You better correct that pretty little language of yours before the baby makes an appearance," Melanie scolded and Alex rolled her eyes.

Melanie took a bite of her sandwich and Alex turned green, looking away. "Maybe," she started sheepishly. "If he's a boy… I could name him…"

"Don't even think about it," Mel cut her off. "You are not naming your baby after your dead best friend/lover."

Alex looked down at her swollen fingers. "How did you know?"

Melanie raised an eyebrow and placed her sandwich down. "Because I know you Ally."

Alex touched her bloated belly. She had a wedding ring hanging on a chain. It probably didn't fit her swollen fingers at the moment. "If it's a girl… what should I name her?" Alex questioned.

Mel shrugged. "You'll know when you see her," she promised.

"Whose baby is it?" I asked Thyme, right as Geoff walked in through the front door and into the kitchen. "Seriously?" I suddenly gasped. "No. Not him. He's just too… I don't know."

"Shh!" Thyme shushed. "I can't hear."

I found myself unable to stand still and I began pacing the kitchen as Geoff kissed Alex on the cheek, as if it was the most natural thing in the world. "Hey babe. How are you feeling?"

Alex grinned and then frowned, throwing her hands to her stomach. A second later, I felt the pain in my belly and I dropped to my knees. "Oh no," I hissed.

"Call an ambulance," Alex got out between ragged breaths and then we both screamed at the same time. "Now!"

The pain became stronger and I found myself writhing in it. "Thyme!" I gasped. "Help me."

"I can't," Thyme said apologetically.

"Damn it!"

Melanie went to call the ambulance. "Shit!" Alex growled, holding her stomach tighter, and Geoff took her hand.

I squeezed my eyes shut and fast-forwarded through the pain. But just like the night when Alex was drunk, it just got worse and I couldn't get up from the ground, finding myself in the hospital. I fast-forwarded again. Worse.

This was worse than when Olivia drowned. It hurt more than when Patrick hit her, threw the bottle at her. It hurt more than the car accident did. I felt sicker than the alcohol made Alex.

I fast-forwarded again.

The pain was dulling but it was throbbing in my abdomen. I cried out and I heard Alex doing the same from somewhere nearby. I couldn't find her though because my eyes were squeezed shut. She clearly did not have any pain medication because this was almost unbearable.

He was walking towards me, his hand outstretched, his fingers extended. His shaggy hair was brushed back. His brown eyes were comforting. I wanted to reach forward and take his hand. He whispered my name and he was gone.

The pain was clearing out and I just felt relief. My body suddenly felt light.

"Alex," Geoff was whispering.

I opened my eyes and I was in a hospital room, much like the one where Alex woke up after the accident. Pam was there.

"Mom?" Alex whispered hoarsely and looked at Pam, then at Melanie who was sitting at the side of the room, then at Geoff who stood next to her bed, holding something in his arms.

It suddenly hit me. I leaned forwards and looked at the small baby. She had Alex's brown eyes and her face. She looked just like her. "We almost lost you there," Pam said.

She looked so much older. Her hair was graying and it was now cut short. She had many wrinkles. But she was still very pretty. "Hey sweetie," she said. "Want to hold your baby?"

Alex peeked up from her medicated gaze and stared at the bundle in Geoff's arms. "Yeah," she croaked.

Geoff leaned down and placed the tiny girl into Alex's arms. The baby settled there, looking content.

"Baby girl," Alex whispered, her words slurred. "What should we name 'er?"

"Something unusual," Geoff said and I saw the thought in Alex eyes.

"Devonne?" she offered and I whispered the name at the same time.

"That's unusual," Geoff agreed. "And very pretty."

Melanie and Pamela frowned and I knew what they are thinking. They knew, and for whatever reason, Geoff didn't. Alex never told him. And now their baby girl was named after a man who died in her arms, and who wasn't Geoff.

Tell Him

"I can't believe you haven't ever told him!" Melanie hissed quietly as soon as Geoff left the room.

"Can we not talk about it right now?" Alex mumbled sleepily, holding her sleeping baby in her arms.

"No! We're talking about it now. You never told him about Devin or how you got those pretty little scars?"

Melanie motioned towards Alex's chest. "He's knows I was in a car accident with a friend when I was younger and that the friend didn't make it."

"Yeah, and did you mention that you were *in love* with said friend *and* that his name was Devin?"

Alex covered Devonne's ears and glared. "Please?" she begged. "Let's just be calm now. Okay?"

Melanie rolled her eyes. "You have a lot of issues Alex. You just had a freaking baby and you still can't forget about someone you liked in *high school*."

Tears filled Alex's eyes. "He was my best friend and I loved him!" she shrieked, just as Geoff walked into the room and gave everyone questioning looks. He was wearing glasses.

"Who was?" Geoff asked.

Thyme had left me here to watch this fighting by myself. I'd definitely had enough of this life.

Melanie looked back and forth as the baby began to cry, and Alex cradled her. "Please," she begged. "Just calm down."

Geoff turned to Melanie and asked her what was going on as Alex hid her face against Devonne. "Her high-school best friend/ love of her life died in that car with her that day. His name was Devin, and Alex never told you about him."

"Get the hell out," Alex hissed in a whisper and the

baby continued to cry as rain began to beat down outside.

"Why didn't you ever tell me?" Geoff asked calmly and Alex just shrugged.

"Because I don't like to talk about it."

"So? I'm your husband. We've been married for four years."

"Okay, *please* stop!" Alex begged as a nurse walked in to see what all the commotion was.

Melanie quickly left the room. Alex held her baby and blocked out the rest of the world.

"We'll talk about this later," Geoff said.

"No," Alex begged and tears ran down her face.

"Alexandra," Geoff said, his voice hard and demanding. "I don't know what you are hiding, but you will tell me."

The bit of makeup that Alex had been wearing earlier was now smudged across her face. She was a mess. Their baby was slowly quieting down.

"I don't have to do anything," Alex said.

Geoff turned and left the room without another word.

Divorce

I was standing in the middle of the old apartment with the cracked paint on the walls. Suitcases were packed and bags stood next to the door. Alex's hair was slightly longer, now below her shoulders. She looks like she'd aged twenty years in the past two.

Devonne walked around the living room, tripping and getting back up. I felt pure love for her as I saw her dark, curly hair, big brown eyes, and pudgy limbs. She was really beautiful, just like Alex was. I wanted to reach out and take the small girl into my arms. I didn't even realize that I was attempting it until my hands went right through her.

I looked up and saw Melanie standing on the side of the room. Despite everything, she was still there for Alex, still her friend.

"That's the last of my stuff," Geoff sighed, walking into the living room where Alex was watching Devonne run around and around.

"I'm sorry that we couldn't make it work," Alex sighed.

Geoff nodded slowly and kneeled down, taking Devonne into his arms. She let him hold her and squirmed slightly. "Dada," she mumbled.

Alex had tears in her eyes and she held her head high as she watched him interact with their daughter. Melanie covered her mouth to hide her own tears.

"I'm sorry too," Geoff said and frowned as he stood.

He placed Devonne back onto the ground and she looked up at him. He turned, collected his things, and left. "Dada?" the young girl cried.

Alex stood and bent down to hold her daughter as she began to wail. "You'll see Daddy during the weekend baby," she comforted and there were tears in her eyes. "I have you now. We'll be okay."

The baby's nose ran and her face was red from the screaming. "Dada!" she cried.

"Mama's here," Alex cooed and she began to cry too, holding the baby to her chest. "Mama's here."

The baby looked up at her mother and stopped crying. "I want Dada," she whispered.

Alex shut her eyes. "I know."

Alone

My head was rushing. I vaguely saw Thyme standing next to me, but I was already merging with Alex and I heard her thoughts in my head.

I lay in bed and thought of my daughter, Devonne, who was now off at college, being an artist, something I used to want to be. I could have been an artist but I let that slip right through my fingers.

I could feel his presence now. He was standing close to me. I was young, yet so old. I'd never met him. He was holding out his hand to me. He was waiting for me.

I rolled over in the warm, smooth sheets and felt myself drifting away. I knew I was almost gone. I had been for a while. I finished what I had to and now I could finally let go.

"I know you can feel it," Thyme whispered from somewhere far away.

I realized that this life was about feeling. There were not many thoughts of living in my head. I'd been living out of it, stuck in some other place. I didn't know where my head had been since that night.

"Just relax," Thyme said. "It's almost over."

My lungs were weak and I knew it. They always had been ever since the accident. I found that it was harder to breathe so I held my breath, waiting. My body forced me to painfully suck in air and I fought against it.

Death would not be scary this time, because I knew the truth.

That night, in the accident, when I watched *him* die, those were the last few seconds of my *real* life.

That night in the accident, I died with him.

Taylor

The second I was able to breathe, I found myself sobbing so hard that it was not even worth trying to stop. Thyme was there, comforting me. Her hand rested on the small of my back and she just waited as I cried. My body was shifting to take on the form of the next life. I felt skinner and bonier. My shoulders were pointy and my fingers were elongated and thin. My hair became long and blond and silky.

I didn't think I could handle this last life. It was too much. The first one was sad. The second one was unbearable. That's why, in this third life, when I heard the crying of someone nearby, I paused it and didn't look up.

My crying was slowly calming down and I wrapped my arms around myself to hold my dead heart in my chest. For the longest time, the silence was all I needed. I hid behind the darkness of my eyelids. "What *are* you?" I whispered to Thyme. "For real this time."

It was quiet for a long time, but I didn't really mind. Even if she didn't answer, I was okay right where I was at this moment. "I'm like you," Thyme finally said, her voice flat.

"Dead?" I asked.

"I guess you could say that."

"You definitely aren't an angel," I concluded. "Angels are sweet. You can be a bitch."

"Yeah," Thyme chuckled darkly. "So I've been told."

"Thyme," I said once again. "Why are you here? Stuck in this world between worlds?"

"Alright," Thyme finally gave in. "I had one life. At the end of each life you have the option of trying again."

"So why did I live three lives?" I asked, suddenly angry at everything and nothing. "My second life was a disaster. Why would I try again?"

"Because you wanted to be happy," Thyme explained and her voice was like music as she spoke. "I guess I always wanted the same thing but... in my life, I was too distraught the entire time. It was a waste. I had nothing. Nobody wanted me. I wanted nobody. I worked in a spice and herb factory and the spices would burn my eyes and sting the cuts on my hands all day long. That's why I go by Thyme. It was endless, just like time is. But the spices were so real and agonizing."

She grasped my hand and the world faded to a very grey one. We were standing in some factory-like place. There were machines, and the smell of spices took me by surprise. I covered my nose. The scent was too strong for me.

Thyme, standing next to me, stared at a young woman who struggled to grind a plant into a powder. There were welts and blisters on her fingers and palms. She hissed as bits of the powder bounced up and into her hands. Tears filled her eyes and she quickly rubbed her hand against her dress to stop the stinging. Somebody yelled "Taylor!" and she quickly went back to work.

Her blond hair fell in her face, hiding the tears that ran down her cheeks. "That's you, isn't it?" I whispered. "Taylor?"

"Yes," Thyme snapped. "Are you happy now Jane Doe? I was a huge failure. I had nothing, no one!"

I inhaled deeply, catching the strong aroma of thyme coming from the powder that Taylor was grinding up. "So what happened?" I questioned.

The world around me shifted, and I saw the same girl, wearing a dress made of scrap fabric, running through the rain, trying to get inside. She landed right into the arms of a man who she slowly backed away from. They apologized to one another, yet neither of them left. They just stood there in the rain, becoming soaked to the bone.

"I met Tommy. He was lovely. He cared about me more than anyone ever had. We were in love."

The scene switched to a hunter walking through the forest, aiming a rifle at a doe. The creature heard the snap of a twig beneath the hunter's foot and turned to run as he pulled the trigger. The deer didn't fall, but Tommy did. Taylor watched as he hit the ground, and she fell to her knees beside him, screaming his name. There was a rifle in his hand. He had been aiming at the same deer.

"He died young," Thyme whispered. "Just like Devin. I hadn't wanted to try again at the end of my life. But… Tommy didn't choose me. He was already with another girl from his past life. So tell me Jane Doe, why would I want to go through that again?"

"To find a deeper love," I offered.

Thyme's eyes were so sad as she said, "There was nothing deeper than what we had, and what we lost."

"You should really try again," I suggested. "Just let this all go and try again."

She looked over at Tommy's face. His eyes were wide and he watched Taylor with a fading gaze. His eyes didn't move again. Taylor hid her face in her hands and sobbed.

"You don't get it," Thyme hissed. "I have no choice. I do what I do now to make others happy. When people find their true love after life, it is because of me and others like me. I love what I do."

I watched her for a long moment and said, "No you don't."

Thyme didn't answer.

Part Three
Mia

I carefully opened my eyes to find that we were in some type of waiting room in a hospital. There was a young woman with blond hair and blue eyes holding a baby, her face frozen in grief.

The baby in her arms had equally blue eyes and blond hair on her head. She was lovely.

I simply said, "Play," and watched as the young woman cried over the baby in her arms.

"It's a great loss," the doctor wearing blue scrubs said. "I am deeply sorry. Having a baby when her body was already so broken from cancer destroyed her."

"Please," the woman begged. "Just go."

The doctor nodded and apologized again before leaving the woman to hold the baby.

"She's way too young to be my mother," I observed.

"That's because she's not your mother Jane Doe. She's your sister."

I didn't respond to Thyme's tired voice. I was allowing her the time to herself that we both knew she needed after revisiting her own sad life.

"Go," I said simply and she didn't hesitate.

The woman with the blond hair sat down in a seat and held the baby close to her. The man next to her asked her what the name of the baby was. For a long moment she hesitated and then said, "Mia, after my mother Maria."

"What a pretty name," the stranger said, and the girl stood and left the hospital, crying the whole way to the front door.

Based on the world outside- the cars and the outfits and the buildings- I knew I was somewhere in the 1990s to the 2000s. The girl caught a taxi and asked the man to take her

to an apartment building in Time Square.
I was in New York.

Katherine

There was no dizziness in this life. The memories were clearer and all of my senses were stronger. I was in a small apartment. Fresh air blew in through the window and engulfed the room. The sun shined brightly outside. Something about this apartment was so familiar.

And then it hit me.

This was Alex's and Geoff's apartment. This woman must have been the next owner of it.

I was currently in a living room with a kitchenette attached to the right of it and a dining room next to that. There were two half-used mugs on the coffee table.

The woman with the blond hair took the baby over to the sofa and sat down, looking at her with tears running down her cheeks. The baby began to cry. "What am I supposed to do?" the girl asked the baby. "I can't take care of you. I can barely take care of myself. You were never supposed to be mine. You were supposed to be our mother's."

The baby screamed louder and the woman rocked her. "Shh. Shh. Come on baby. Stop crying," she begged and looked up at the ceiling, as if to ask for help. "Please," she whispered. "Baby Mia, please."

She looks up at the kitchen and said, "You're hungry, aren't you?"

She warmed up some formula for Mia, who started to drink it and quieted down. The woman sighed deeply and slid down to the ground, holding the baby. "We'll be okay," she tried to promise. "My name is Katherine. Most people call me Kat. I'm sixteen years old." She choked slightly and could barely get the words out. "I'm your sister."

Moving

I flashed forward. It must have been about a month later. The baby was still a baby and Kat looked exactly the same, just a bit more together as she moved around the apartment and packed things away. Another girl walked into the room. She had red hair and purple lipstick. "Kat," she said, carrying a huge box. "Are you really sure about this?"

"Yeah," Kat sighed. "I need this. It's better for the both of us to just start fresh. You know what I mean Stephanie?"

"I guess," Stephanie lied, placing down the box she was holding. "I just don't get you. You grew up here."

"And now I'm leaving," Kat responded. "Look, I've made up my mind, okay?"

Her hair was pulled back and she wore jeans and a t-shirt with a coffee stain on it. She held a sleeping Mia.

"Can we stop talking and keep packing?" Kat asked, and Stephanie nodded.

"How on earth are you going to raise a baby all by yourself?" she asked, totally ignoring what Kat had just said.

"That's why I'm moving up to Maine, where my aunt and uncle live. They can help me out."

Kat placed Mia on a blanket in the middle of the living room.

The two continued to pack for a long time and finally a horn honked downstairs. "That's Max," Kat said. "And that's the last of these boxes. Thanks Steph."

Stephanie looked at her friend and then hugged her tightly. "Good luck," she whispered. "Take good care of that baby. Don't let her turn out all crazy."

"I'll do my best," Kat laughed, but there were tears in her eyes as she pulled away, collected the baby and the blanket, and was on her way.

Maine

"Aunt Luuuuccccccy!" a little girl with long blond hair, bangs, and blue eyes shouted as she ran down the old wooden steps of a small house.

There were pictures all over the turquoise walls, and furniture decorating the hallway, filling up the little space the house had to offer.

"Aunt Luuuuuccccccccy!" the girl shouted again.

"Child," an older, graying woman stopped her. "Relax. I heard you the first time. No more hot cocoa for you."

The little blond-haired girl started bouncing all over the place. "No. I'm sorry. Don't take it away, please."

Lucy relaxed slightly. "What can I help you with?" she asked, kneeling down to the child's level.

"I um… was wondering um… if you could um… make me some pancakes with syrup and chocolate chips," Mia stammered out.

I laughed quietly, actually remembering the smell of the melting chocolate and sugary pancakes baking in the kitchen. Even now, when I couldn't eat, my mouth watered for the pancakes that Lucy made.

"Because that's just what you need. More sugar," Lucy said sarcastically.

"Pleeeeaaassse!" Mia begged, jumping up and down again.

Suddenly, somebody walked down the stairs and tired eyes met Lucy's. "Mornin' Lucy," Kat yawned. "Mimi, what are you doing up so early?"

Mia made a face, trying to look incredibly grown-up. "It is not early. It is eleven o'clock and you slept in, Kitty-Kat."

Kat chuckled, but she was clearly a mess. Her hair was a bird's nest around her head and there were dark bags under her eyes. "Did you eat?"

"No," Mia said, folding her arms over her chest. "Aunt Lucy doesn't wanna make me pancakes."

Kat looked sadly at Lucy and murmured, "I'll make 'em."

Lucy sighed deeply. "Yay!" Mia squealed.

She quickly turned and ran up the stairs, giggling the whole way there. "You," Lucy sighed, pointing a finger at Kat. "Have got to stop giving the girl whatever she wants like *that*." She snapped her fingers.

"My mom used to make me pancakes every morning," Kat said flatly and walked right past her into the kitchen.

The walls of the kitchen were very modern, but very old as well. There was a crack running up the wall. Kat pulled her hair up and tied it behind her head. She walked out of an old screen door into a backyard where a loud, banging sound was heard. "Well it's about time you got up," an older, heavier man said as Kat walked outside.

"Hey Stanley," Kat greeted. "I just heard you out here. I was wondering what was going on."

"I was chopping down firewood."

"You know they sell that right down the street?" Kat reminded him and he just stared.

"I ain't giving no money when I don't got to."

"Yeah okay."

Kat rolled her eyes and worked her way back into the house. "And what're you up to?" Stanley called after her.

She turned around and shivered as a wind touched her bare arms. It was then that I noticed the fuzzy slippers she wore. "I'm making pancakes for my sister."

"Mhm," Stanley hummed.

"What's that supposed to mean?" Kat demanded.

"It means you've got that little girl on a pedestal. She's gonna turn up all spoiled if you don't watch yourself."

Kat's lip quivered slightly and she blinked fast. "I

didn't 'turn up all spoiled' and my mom treated me the same way."

"Katherine, your mamma was a good woman. But she was careful with you. She made you a smart lady. You're all grown now, even though you weren't ready to be grown so fast. Now start treating that girl like a person and not the queen of the world."

"I'm making her breakfast! I don't want her to starve."

"And what in the world is wrong with oatmeal or grits? You just woke up."

"She doesn't like oatmeal or grits."

Stanley sighed deeply, and stepped away from the broken down tree that he had been whacking with an axe. "You're her guardian. You need to put your foot down. She's your family."

Kat narrowed her eyes. "She's all I have left. I don't need to lose her too."

Right as she walked inside, Stanley said, "You've got us darlin'."

Regression

As my vision adjusted, I was standing in a dark bedroom. It was hard to make out anything except a bed and a person sleeping in it. Rain was pounding down outside the house as lightning flashed brightly.

Suddenly, a figure came running in through the bedroom door as thunder boomed loudly. "Kat!" a voice gasped in a whisper as hands shook the person in the bed.

The woman woke up slowly. "What's wrong?"

"It's raining really hard," a tiny, fearful voice said.

The woman sat up and turned her bedside lamp on. Mia must have been around sixteen, a surprising age to still be afraid of thunderstorms. "Come on," Kat sighed, pulling the blankets aside and making room.

Mia's blond hair was a mess. Her big blue eyes were pretty much equal to those of her sister's. They looked exactly the same. Mia, wearing fuzzy pajama pants and a t-shirt, climbed into bed beside her sister and curled up next to her. They turned the lights off. Thunder blasted again and Mia nearly jumped from the bed. "It's alright," Kat whispered, automatically wrapping her arms around her, as if they've done this many times before.

"Aunt Lucy says that... never mind..." Mia trailed off.

The darkness of the tiny room flashed to light and Kat grasped Mia's hand. "What?" she whispered. "What does Lucy say?"

"She says..." Mia sighed and leaned further back against the pillow. "She thinks I'm scared of the rain because of something in a past life."

I gasped and backed up, nearly falling straight through the wall, which was bad because this wall would lead me two stories down to the ground that I couldn't even feel.

"That's ridiculous," Kat said quickly, and although she was fast to put down the idea, I couldn't help but love her.

"Go back to sleep Mimi."

"It's not that ridiculous," Thyme said, and I knew she was back as long as I was willing to drop the subject of her life.

"Where's Anita/ Pam in this life?" I suddenly whispered, knowing that something huge had been missing ever since I've started watching this.

"Her life cycle finished after her last life. She didn't choose another life," Thyme explained, her voice emotionless.

"But w-why... I mean her husband *died*. Why wouldn't she want to see him again in another life?"

"Because her wish came true." Thyme shrugged.

"And how would you know?" I asked, looking around the now silent room.

"Because I was her guide," Thyme answered softly. "She didn't need another life. Her wishes came true when she had you as her daughter. So in your last life, you are left with no mother. Just your sister."

I stared in the dark at the figure next to Mia. Tears were in my eyes and I swallowed the thick lump in my throat. "Is Kat Melanie?" I guessed, trying to change the subject to something I could talk about without crying, and Thyme nodded slowly. "Which would make her in my first life-"

"Emily," Thyme interrupted, finishing for me. "You'd be surprised how many times a person can make an appearance in our lives. Emily was always meant to be your best friend, and your sister."

I felt tears in my eyes again. Soft, faded memories of my sister entered my mind and I smiled.

I blinked and I was standing in the kitchen again. Even though it was years later from the first time I'd seen it, it hadn't changed at all, except for some extra stains and a leak in the ceiling. Mia slowly entered the kitchen and she was fully dressed in a t-shirt and jeans. Lucy looked much older. Her hair was fully white now. But her face was still very pretty.

"Okay," Mia said, sounding as if she was giving in. "Let's do this."

Lucy nodded and grabbed two raincoats, handing one to Mia. As Lucy went outside with an umbrella, Mia paused for a long moment before following her through the rain, careful to stay beneath the umbrella.

I closed my eyes and when I opened them, I was in a building that I had never seen before. It was incredibly small. It was mainly one large waiting room and a smaller room in the back. Beads divided the two areas and I struggled to see past them to the darkness that seemed to glow. A woman with dreadlocks and dark skin walked out, looking slightly satisfied yet on edge all at once.

"Next," an older, raspy voice came from the other room.

I felt my stomach jump uncomfortably and I looked up to see that Mia was breathing quickly. "Maybe this is a bad idea," she said to Lucy but as the rain picked up outside, she looked even more afraid.

"Go," Lucy coxed. "It'll be worth it in the long run."

"Next!" the voice called again, irritated.

Mia kissed Lucy on the cheek and then slowly made her way into the room. The beaded strings ran along her skin softly and fell back into place, dangling after she'd moved them. I followed her in as Lucy resituated herself in the waiting room.

The next room was very dark and candles were the only thing illuminating it. There were odd cards and plants that I had never seen before lining the room. There was even a crystal ball on the side of the small, round table that sat in the middle of the room. A middle-aged woman was sitting in a chair with a cushion, waiting for Mia to take the wooden chair without a cushion that sat on the other side.

Mia slowly sat down and placed her hands in her lap. "What can I help you with?" the woman asked in her raspy voice with a slight accent to it that I couldn't place.

Smoke from one candle rose up and surrounded the room. "I was wondering if... maybe you could tell me about my past lives."

"Obviously I can. It's what you want to know about them that is the key," the woman said, easily losing her patience.

"So... have I had past lives?"

The woman sighed and closed her eyes. She reached her hands out and instructed Mia to place her hands inside her own. Mia's hands were young and beautiful compared to the old, dry looking ones of the woman. I noticed that the room smelled of unnatural fragrances. The woman inhaled deeply and her shoulders rose with her breath. As she slowly let it out Mia began to shake slightly in fear. "Yes," the woman said. "Two past lives. This is your third."

Mia looked taken aback and my mouth had fallen straight open. This wasn't just some fake hoax. This was the real deal. Crazy, Creepy Lady actually knew what the heck she was talking about. "Is that all?" she asked.

"Well... no," Mia said. "I um... I've heard that you can define fears and feelings from one life based on your past, and I'm scared of rain."

"So you want to know what is causing it," Crazy confirmed.

Mia nodded slowly.

"Close your eyes," the woman said and Mia looked alarmed. "Don't be afraid," the woman said. "I can feel heartbeat from over here. It's beating very fast. You need to calm it down if I am going to hypnotize you."

"Hypnotize?" Mia gasped, automatically leaning away in her chair.

"Yes. If you want to remember your past life then you

must do it yourself." The woman told her to close her eyes and she finally gave in, shutting them softly. "Now picture yourself in a dark tunnel."

Mia nodded her head quickly. "Okay," she said.

"Not okay," Creepy responded. "If you were really there, you wouldn't seem so anxious. Breathe deeply for a long moment and relax. When you are in the tunnel, I will give you the next step. I will be able to tell when you are ready."

Mia swallowed thickly and tried to calm her breathing. I watched for a moment as she tapped her fingers against her leg and continued to breathe quickly. But slowly, she began to calm down and her breathing slowed. A faint picture of a tunnel was in my head and I closed my eyes, seeing it become clearer, stretched out before me, as Mia saw it.

"Now," a voice instructed. "Picture a light wrapping around you. See the most beautiful light you can think of. It is your protection. Carry it with you and walk through the tunnel and let it take you to where you need to go. On the other side of the tunnel it is raining. But do not be alarmed, the rain cannot hurt you. It is only there to guide you. If at any time during this process, you feel unsafe, go back to the tunnel. You are safe there."

I walked forwards through the tunnel, wrapped in a blanket of beautiful, white light that covered me. It was raining on the other side of the tunnel. I began to walk towards it, seeing a flash of lightning that nearly held me back. But I pushed forwards again.

There was a flash of something besides lightning and I was in a warm enclosed area and the rain surrounded me but didn't touch me. I was not alone. There was a presence beside me.

Fear pulsed through me and I went back to the tunnel. The rain was now pouring on the other side of it. I relaxed slightly, remembering that the rain couldn't hurt me.

"What did you see?" a voice asked, and I could hear Mia answering that she was in a car with a man.

"What is the year?" the voice asked but Mia didn't respond.

Slowly I walked back towards the rain and felt as the world flashed again through lightning to me waking up in pain on the side of the road, alone in a car.

I flashed back to the tunnel and heard as Mia recounted what we just saw. The voice told her to continue on her journey and see what else was happening. Slowly the rain intensified. I walked towards it, afraid of what I might see.

I was on the side of the road, holding him in my arms, begging him to stay with me. I collapsed forward. He was gone.

My eyes snapped open and Mia's did too. I caught my breath, knowing exactly what I just saw. That was the night Devin died. Mia gasped harshly and stood up.

"I can't do this," she said suddenly as tears entered her eyes.

"You can never solve the problem if you don't know why it was caused," Crazy explained.

"Look," Mia snapped. "I don't wanna know what it was caused by. All I know is that it was really bad and it was meant to stay in a past life. It's over now."

"Then why are you still afraid of rain?" Creepy demanded.

Mia wiped her tears quickly. "That's my business," she said. "How much do I owe you?"

The woman sighed deeply. "Consider this one on me," she said. "I'm sorry I couldn't help you."

Mia nodded slowly and practically bolted from the room. I followed her, feeling as if the walls were about to close in on me. If my heart was beating, it would be going a mile a minute.

Lucy stood the second Mia walked over to her. "How'd it go?"

"Let's get out of here," Mia demanded. "Now please! Let's just go! Aunt Lucy please!"

"Okay, okay," Lucy said, grabbing Mia's hand and pulling her from the building.

When they got outside, the rain had just stopped and Mia breathed in deeply, looking relieved.

"That was *intense*," Thyme said and I gasped, still on edge.

"Yeah," I agreed. "It really was. Did you just get here?"

"Sort of. I saw everything."

"I'm sure you did."

Neighbors

Mia held Kat's arm tightly as they made their way next door and stopped in front of the house. Mia was holding a basket in her hand. Lucy wasn't far behind them. Mia squeezed Kat's hand really hard and gasped when Kat knocked on the door. "What is going on with you?" Kat demanded.

"Nothing," Mia murmured. "I'm fine."

The door swung open and she jumped. A woman with long dark hair and brown eyes stood on the other side of the door with what looked to be her husband. She had a friendly smile. "Hi," Lucy said, finally making her way up to the door. "We heard that we had some new neighbors and we wanted to give you a proper welcome."

"Oh!" the woman gasped. "How nice. Michael!"

A man with blond hair appeared next to her a few seconds later. His belly was huge and bloated. I looked to see that Thyme was watching from a distance. "Hello," Michael said. "You must be our neighbors."

Lucy elbowed Kat who elbowed Mia who quickly held the basket up in front of her. "This is for you," Mia said, forcing a big smile.

"Oh how thoughtful!" the woman said and took the basket. "My name is Kimberly and this is Michael. We have a son, but he's sleeping right now."

"It's two in the afternoon," Lucy chuckled.

"Well he's a teenage boy and he stayed up late last night. I really should wake him up in a few minutes. In fact… I'm about to go do that."

Mia smiled slightly and looked up at Kat who said, "I'm uh Kat. And this is my sister Mia, and my aunt Lucy."

They all gave a smile. "Well thank you so much for the welcoming basket. We would love to invite you over sometime for dinner."

"That would be lovely," Lucy said and they all said goodbye before the door shut and Mia's smile fell.

"What is wrong with you?" Kat demanded.

"It's nothing," Mia lied and looked up to Lucy for help.

Kat narrowed her eyes.

Balconies

"You did what?" Kat shrieked and it was the first thing I heard as I appeared in the kitchen.

"Aunt Lucy took me to see a psychic," Mia said slowly. Her blond hair was tied back and her blue eyes were red from crying.

"Well no wonder you're so freaked out! Lucy is in for quite an earful when I get my hands on her!"

"Stop it!" Mia cut her off. "Katie please. Look, I know you said not to go but I had to try. And now I don't wanna go back. It was all phony-baloney stuff. None of it was real," Mia lied. "It was just creepy, okay? And I don't wanna talk about it."

"Fine," Kat snapped, standing up to put her plate in the sink. "Suit yourself. But don't come crying to me when you start having all kinds of nightmares."

"I'll be fine!" Mia shrieked. "I'm fifteen years old! I won't be having any nightmares!"

"We'll see," Kat snapped and stomped up the stairs.

Mia threw her fork down and left it at the table, flouncing up the stairs as well. She entered her room and slammed the door shut behind her. Thyme and I followed her closely. Thyme was barely talking now, just allowing me to watch. She opened her mouth to say something and I automatically shushed her. Mia pulled open a door on the wall across from us and it revealed a balcony that I didn't even know she had.

"May I speak now Jane Doe?" Thyme asked and I shook my head. "Come on! We are just getting to the good part. Ooh watch this!"

"Shut it!" I hissed and pushed her out of the way, but I secretly smiled.

I kind of liked spending time with her, although I would

never admit it to her face.

"I always wonder what's going on inside that head of yours," Thyme whispered, shaking her head back and forth.

"I bet you do," I teased and rolled my eyes.

Something hit the ground from down below and Mia gasped, leaning over the railing to see what it was. She leaned further and further, and for a moment I was afraid she was going to fall. But then a voice surprised the both of us.

"You're not going to jump are you?" a male voice said.

Mia gasped and tripped backwards, catching her balance by grasping the railing. She looked over to find a boy, around her age, standing on the balcony next to hers. He was average height and had brown hair and brown eyes. His hair was wavy and fell just past his neck. He was cute like Patrick, but not as 'pretty boy' and he almost looked a little 'bad boy,' but not as much as Devin. I liked him already and I hadn't even learned his name yet.

"Gosh no!" Mia breathed. "For heaven's sake… I would never! Who are you anyway?"

The boy chuckled lightly and reached his hand across the balconies. "Lucas," he introduced and held his hand out, waiting for Mia to shake it. I whispered his name silently, a mantra on my lips. "And you are?"

"Mia," she responded and slowly took his hand. "You must be the new neighbors."

"Well one of them at least," Lucas teased and Mia raised an eyebrow as he pulled his hand away. "It's nice to meet you Mia."

"You too," she sighed and looked down again over the ledge. "Did you see something fall before?"

"Oh, you mean the rock I threw?" Lucas offered.

Mia backed up and just stared at him, a small smile playing on her lips. "You just threw a rock? For fun?"

"Give it a try," Lucas said and grasped a rock from the

ground of his balcony, tossing it over to Mia who clumsily caught it.

"You want me to throw this?"

"No I want you to eat it," Lucas said sarcastically. Mia eyed him and then pretended she was about to put it in her mouth. "No! I was only kidding!"

Mia laughed out loud. "I know," she giggled. "And you should have seen your face."

"So she has a personality?" Lucas muttered as Mia chucked the rock over the ledge and watched it slam into a tree. "Jesus. Nice arm!"

Mia flexed her muscles. "I do try to work out every now and then," she teased and Lucas tossed over another rock, watching it land at her feet.

"Rock tossing contest?" he offered, picking one up for himself.

"Oh, you are on!" Mia gasped and grabbed the rock from the ground.

"One."

"Two."

"Three!" they both shouted and threw the rocks over the edge.

Both rocks went flying into the trees and I couldn't help laughing as I sunk down to the ground and watched. "I won!" Mia announced.

"Oh no! I *so* won! It's obvious! Didn't you see where my rock hit?"

"Don't even try and trick me. I-"

"*Mia!*" a voice yelled and the two of them stopped speaking. "What on earth are you doing?"

"Nothing!" Mia shouted back, her eyes narrowing automatically.

"You know you aren't supposed to talk to strangers!" the voice responded. I sighed deeply when I realized that it was Kat's voice. "Who are you talking to?"

"No one!" Mia lied. "I'm talking to myself!"

Mia looked over at Lucas and smiles apologetically. "Sorry," she whispered to him. "Unfortunately you are a stranger and I shouldn't be talking to you."

Lucas chuckled and nodded. "Alright fine," he sighed. "But I won that contest."

Mia rolled her eyes. "Goodbye Lucas. I'll see you later."

She turned and walked into the house. I followed her and we both gasped when we found Lucy waiting in her room. "No one?" Lucy questioned. "He sure seemed like someone to me."

Mia looked horror struck and Lucy laughed quietly. "Please don't tell Kat," Mia begged.

"What's it worth to ya?" Lucy teased.

"I'll do the laundry tomorrow?" Mia responded like a question and I groaned. *I hate laundry.*

"You've got yourself a deal."

Lucy winked and left the room. Mia fell backwards onto her bed and sighed. "Who was he?" I asked Thyme.

"Lucas. Weren't you paying attention?"

"You know that's not what I meant," I threw back. "I mean… is he the love interest of this life… or one of many?"

Thyme shrugged. "Guess you'll have to find out."

"But Mia's so young," I said when I decided that Lucas was exactly who I thought he was. "So help me if I die young one more time…"

"Then what? It's already happened if that's the truth. There's nothing you can do about it now. You lived until your early fifties in your last life and your late thirties in the life before that. Guess you'll only know more about this life if you shut your mouth and watch."

"Of all the people that could help me out," I muttered. "I get stuck with you."

"Oh I'm fabulous. You could have gotten stuck with some lonely old man who died of natural causes and was bored. There are plenty of those."

"And how did you die?" I asked, knowing I was crossing a line I shouldn't be.

Thyme frowned and turned away from me. "Happiness can get to your head Jane Doe. You're never prepared to lose it. I lost it and found myself lonely for a long, long time until a fire turned it all to ashes."

"I'm really sorry Thyme," I finally said. "Tommy's an idiot for not choosing you. He really is."

"Aren't we all?" Thyme muttered and flashed me a half-hearted smile.

Star-Gazing

It was nighttime when my vision adjusted and I was once again standing on the balcony outside of Mia's room. Thyme was sitting next to me, but she refused to say a word. Finally, Lucas's door opened and he waltzed outside. He waited a long moment, staring right through me to Mia's balcony, until Mia's door finally creaked open and Mia tip-toed out. I could tell some time had passed; Mia's bangs were growing out. It was very cold outside and Mia shivered, holding a jacket tightly around her. Lucas was wearing a heavy sweatshirt.

"Finally," Lucas whispered. "Happy birthday."

"Yeah," Mia sighed. "Thanks."

"Is something wrong?"

"It's nothing," Mia assured him, quickly smiling. "Now show me another constellation."

Lucas chuckled and lay down on the ground of his balcony and Mia did the same. "Look up at the sky," Lucas said.

"I'm looking," Mia mumbled, peeking over at Lucas's face.

"At the sky," Lucas reminded her and she giggled, doing as she was told.

I found myself looking up as well and relaxing to the heavy sound of both Lucas's and Mia's breathing. "Let's see… look up at Aquarius, the one I showed you last night."

Mia's eyes traveled up to the stars and slowly skimmed the sky until she nodded. "Found it," she whispered. "Now what?"

"Look at the stars below it and to the right, just under the legs of Aquarius. Do you see that bigger star near the left foot of Aquarius?"

Mia squinted for a moment and then sighed, "Mhm."

"Follow that line. That's the horn of the animal. Follow it over two stars to the right and then move your eyes down to the next star below it. Follow that to the right to a clump of stars. Do you see it?"

"I think so." Mia was now tracing the sky with her finger, one eye open and the other eye shut.

Lucas peeked over at her and smirked. "You are now at the jaw of the animal. Now move that line two stars up and then connect it to the other side of the face. Do you see the whole face now?"

Mia smiled. "Yeah."

"Now if you look to the right of that, you will see the body of the animal; the tail, the legs, and the torso."

"I see it!" Mia suddenly gasped in a whisper.

Lucas chuckled. "Can you guess what kind of animal it is?"

Mia made a face and squinted her eyes. "A dog? A bird maybe? But neither of those have horns. An elephant? No there's no big ears. A goat?" And then she paused as it sunk in.

"Capricornus; better known as Capricorn- your zodiac sign. It's half goat, half fish," Lucas explained and Mia was pressing her lips together. Lucas looked over at her and his eyes widened. "Why are you crying?"

Mia quickly wiped away her tears. "It's nothing. I just... never thought I'd get to see it in the sky. It's incredible."

She turned to Lucas and they both just stared at each other. They both sat up. "You really are something," Lucas mumbled slowly and then the tears fell faster down Mia's face. "Aw Mia. What's the matter? You were crying when you first came outside."

"It's stupid," Mia got out through her tears and wiped them away quickly. "It's just... I always thought that by my sixteenth birthday that some boy would at least be interested in me. But it's never happened. At school I make myself look like a fool in front of boys. Not one of them has even looked my way. I had this crazy wish that by sixteen years old at least someone would kiss me. But even I should have known that wasn't going to happen."

Lucas's face was now troubled and he stood. Mia had hidden her face in her hands. I gasped as Lucas suddenly hoisted himself up and climbed over the edge of his balcony. He reached across to Mia's and pulled himself over it, all in one swift move. Mia held in a scream as Lucas landed on her balcony.

"How did you..." she trailed off, staring at him with wide eyes.

Lucas kneeled down next to her and lifted her chin so she'd look at him, moving his thumb across her cheek. "You're too hard on yourself," he whispered. "Those boys at your school don't know what they're missing out on." Mia looked up through teary eyes and Lucas was still holding her face. "You wanted to be kissed by your sixteenth birthday?" he asked and Mia nodded slowly, as if in a trance. "How's a day late work for ya?"

Mia tilted her head to the side, slightly confused. Lucas leaned forwards and softly brushed his lips against Mia's. She froze and Lucas stood. "Goodnight Mia." He smiled softly. "Happy birthday."

He left her sitting there on the balcony as he climbed back over to his and disappeared into his room. Mia shyly touched her lips and then pulled her jacket tightly around her, stepping back into her own room.

"And that's where it starts," Thyme sighed, mock-dreamily.

"Screw you," I hissed at her and followed Mia into her room.

Bruises

"What's got you in such a happy mood?" Kat asked Mia as she joined her at the breakfast table.

"Nothing," Mia sighed, twirling her hair around her finger.

"Okay, what's gotten into you?" Kat demanded. "And what's going on between you and that boy next door?"

Mia's eyes went wide and then she smiled softly. "I think he might like me," she said.

"Why? Because you have conversations across your balconies?" Kat teased and Mia frowned slightly.

"No," Mia said proudly as she angrily stood from the table and brought her dish to the sink. "Actually because he kissed me."

Kat choked on a sip of orange juice. "He what?" Kat gasped.

Mia banged her shoulder on the wall as she left the kitchen and she cursed under her breath. She headed for the stairs and Kat was quick to follow behind her. I noticed that Mia was limping.

"Did you hurt yourself?" Kat asked.

"It's just a bruise," Mia assured her.

Mia quickly slipped into her room and slammed the door shut behind her, locking it. She yanked off the pajamas she was wearing and went to change into some jeans and a t-shirt. When she slipped out of her pants I noticed the darkened bruise on her knee. There was a huge one across her back as well. Mia cringed as she pulled a shirt on, and I knew that it was not just a bruise.

"What the hell are those?" I asked Thyme. "Is Lucas hitting her like Patrick hit Olivia?"

"Of course not. He only kissed her," Thyme reminded me.

There was a tapping sound coming from the window just as Mia finished changing and she pulled the curtain back, gasping when she saw Lucas standing there. "Hey," he said when she opened the window.

"What is he? A stalker?" I muttered.

"Is it really *that* hard for you to believe that there may not always be something wrong with the guys you date?" Thyme asked pointedly.

I shrugged, narrowing my eyes as Mia whispered, "Hi."

Then she leaned out her window and kissed him suddenly. He was taken by surprise, but he kissed her back. "So he climbs her balcony," I muttered. "If he's not a stalker then he's freaking Romeo."

"First of all *Juliet*, he jumped to her balcony. There's a difference. Second of all, I'm sorry that your last life wasn't so fair to you. Life's not fair!"

Mia pulled back finally when a raindrop fell from the sky and landed on the balcony. "What's wrong?" Lucas asked as the rain began to fall faster, melting the murky snow below.

"Come in," Mia suddenly said. "It must be cold out there."

A rain drop touched her hand and she gasped, wiping it off immediately. "Are you scared of a little rain?" Lucas chuckled and climbed inside, shutting the window behind him.

"Maybe. Just keep it down," Mia warned him and leaned in to kiss him again, silencing him from saying anything more.

Lucas's hand brushed over Mia's shoulder and she cringed. He quickly pulled away. "What's wrong?"

"Nothing. I just hurt my shoulder earlier. That's all."

"Can I take a look?" Lucas asked and Mia shrugged, sliding the sleeve of her shirt over her shoulder. "Mia," Lucas gasped and she shushed him. "You have a huge bruise on your shoulder," he said in a whisper.

I looked at her shoulder and saw the already darkened bruise from where she'd hit it in the kitchen.

Something wasn't not right.

Talking

"Favorite hobby?" Lucas asked and Mia wrapped a blanket tightly around her.

I was standing on the balcony next to Mia. "Singing," she whispered, shivering in the blanket. "I've always wanted to be a singer. How about you?"

"Call me a nerd, but I've always loved reading."

"That's not nerdy. It's cute," Mia giggled, shivering again.

Lucas sighed and jumped over to her balcony, pulling her into his arms right away. He sunk down to the ground and she cuddled against him. "Favorite color?" he murmured quietly.

"Pink."

"Typical," Lucas teased.

"It was the color of my mom's favorite shirt. Kat gave it to me."

"Oh," Lucas said simply. "I'm sorry. I didn't mean…"

"It's fine." Mia smiled. "What's your favorite color?"

"Green. I don't know why. I just like it." Mia laughed softly. "Your turn to come up with a question," Lucas said.

"Why did you guys decide to move here?" Mia asked suddenly.

Lucas frowned slightly. "My parents are never quite happy with where we are living. They move all the time, always wanting something new. I never really have a chance to make friends because of it. I've never had a *real* relationship until now."

"Is that what this is?" Mia whispered. "A relationship?"

"I thought it was," Lucas responded.

"Yeah," Mia giggled, shivering harder. "Me too."

She tugged the blanket tighter around her and I noticed a dark bruise on her hand.

Dark

"Where are we?" I asked as my eyes adjusted to see Mia and Lucas walking hand in hand on a sunny day down a beach.

When I finally adjusted, I noticed that Mia looked slightly older and Lucas did too. He had more muscle and his shoulders were broader. Mia looked a lot thinner and exhausted. She must have be depressed or something.

"What's up with you lately?" Lucas asked as Mia shivered slightly.

"Nothing. I'm just tired."

"You're always tired Mi. You just aren't looking so good lately. Maybe you should see a doctor or something."

Mia pulled her hand away, folding it under her arm. "I'm fine," she insisted.

"Whatever you say," Lucas sighed.

"Mercy," Mia whispered and Lucas dropped the subject. "It's a stupid fight. Just let it go."

"You're right," Lucas agreed. "I used that one on you last week. It's only fair."

"You *are* the one who came up with the idea for a 'special word' to say if we're ever fighting." Mia elbowed him very lightly and smiled, but I noticed that she cringed. Lucas was sweating and Mia pulled her sweater tighter around her. "My sister's from New York," Mia said, starting a new topic.

Lucas nodded slowly. "I've always wanted to go to New York," he said.

"Me too. We should go one day. Just the two of us. We can just take off for New York and never look back."

Lucas frowned. "Mi, you're really starting to concern me."

"Don't be concerned," Mia sighed and Lucas pulled her

into a hug. "I'm fine. I'm with you. I've just always wanted to see New York."

"So maybe we'll go one day," Lucas shrugged as Mia leaned against him.

"It's weird. I've never seen New York but it seems so familiar. Maybe I lived there in a past life."

Mia's eyes were slightly red, but not from crying. She had dark circles under them.

"Do you believe in past lives?" Lucas asked, suddenly serious.

"I think so," Mia shrugged. "I don't actually know."

Lucas smiled softly and his eyes reminded me of the sweet darkness that lived inside of Devin's. Yet he was always quick to see the bright side of things, like Patrick. He was practically a mix of the two. "Maybe we knew each other in a past life," Lucas said.

"We must have," Mia replied. "I feel like I've known you forever." She slowly pulled back and stared up at his face. "We must be like soul mates or something."

"Must be," Lucas agreed and then fell silent for a long time. "I think we are."

"Yeah," Mia whispered hoarsely. "I think so too."

Lucas kissed her head and sighed deeply. "I love you Mi."

My eyes went wide and my heart reached out for Lucas to hold me and comfort me forever. I waited to hear Mia say it back, and Lucas seemed to also. But when she said nothing, he looked heartbroken.

"Mi?" he whispered, shaking her lightly. "Mia?"

He looked down and his eyes went wide when he realized that the only things holding Mia up right now were his arms. She was no longer conscious.

Everything went black.

Mercury

I was swimming somewhere far under the ocean. Everything was beautiful and deep. There was someone waiting for me, holding their hand out. The sunset was shining high above, protecting me from anything that may try to get in the way of me and him. But the water was thick like mercury, like blood. I tried to pull myself through it and I gasped it in as the man holding his hand out to me disappeared and I woke up in a hospital bed, staring at the bright fluorescent lights above me.

I separated myself from Mia's mind and watched from a distance. Mia slowly let her eyes drift shut again. There was a nurse standing next to her, checking her vitals and feeding an IV into her arm. She said Mia's name softly, but stopped when she realized that Mia was asleep again. Lucas was nowhere in sight. The door to the room burst open and Kat ran in with Lucy and Stanley right behind her. "Was she awake yet?" Kat gasped and Mia groaned sleepily.

Kat sat down in the chair next to Mia and the nurse filled her in on some medical information, but told her that she must wait until the doctor could tell her the rest. All she could tell them was that Mia had been in and out of consciousness since she arrived to the hospital.

As she slowly opened her eyes again and saw Kat, Mia didn't seem surprised. "Hey," she mumbled.

Kat just looked at her for a long moment and then she cried, hiding her face against her hands. Mia stared in my direction, and if I didn't know any better, I would think she was looking right at me. But she wasn't.

She was staring at the doctor who held her test results and had the most unreadable expression in his eyes.

Between Kat's crying and Lucy and Stanley's worrying, I couldn't take it anymore.

Lies

I blinked and reappeared outside of Mia's house. She was wearing sweatpants and a sweatshirt and she looked totally exhausted. She hugged her sweatshirt tightly to her. I could faintly feel the pain and nausea that Mia was feeling, and I shuddered. But I must have been quite an actress in my past life, because when Lucas turned the corner and saw her, Mia smiled brightly and pushed the pain behind a wall that Lucas couldn't see through. "Oh thank God!" Lucas gasped and hugged Mia tightly.

There were tears in Mia's eyes as she pulled back and stared at him. "Lucas," she whispered and he touched her face softly.

"What is it? What do you have? Are you gonna be okay?" Lucas asked in one breath and Mia blinked rapidly.

"Yeah, just an untreated virus. I'm going to be fine," Mia got out and tears finally made their way down her face.

Lucas hugged her tightly and she squeezed her eyes shut, resting her head against his chest. "You had me so worried," Lucas whispered. "I was so afraid I was going to lose you."

"Lucas," Mia repeated and he slowly backed up as Mia pressed her hands against his chest. She was now shaking with tears. "I can't... We can't... I have a lot going on right now Lucas," she got out.

"I know," Lucas murmured.

"Shh," Mia stopped him. "Just let me talk okay?" she said quickly. "We're moving."

"What?"

"We um... I think we forced us. I realized... I haven't been completely honest with myself. I don't... I can't..."

"You're breaking up with me," Lucas said, shocked. He wrapped his hands around her shoulders and she cringed. "Mia, we can make us work. Even if you're moving. No matter where you go, I will love you."

"Lucas," Mia stopped him. "I'm sorry. But I can't. I never loved you. And we can't be together."

"What are you doing?" I shrieked, and I knew she was lying.

All of this was a lie! Every single word of it! Who was making her say this? It was ridiculous! It was untrue!

"You're a good guy and you deserve someone who will love you as much as you love them." Now she was sobbing. "I'm so sorry Lucas," Mia choked out. "I'm sorry. I have enough going on. I don't need a relationship too. So you just keep being you because you're amazing. We just were never meant to be."

Lucas's eyes were incredibly wide and hurt and I launched myself at Mia, falling straight through her and landing in front of Thyme's feet. She rolled her eyes and helped me up. "That won't work," she assured me.

Mia kissed Lucas's cheek and then turned, rushing back into her house.

Lucas stood there, stunned.

I followed Mia into her house, angrily trying to figure out what the hell she had just done. But I froze when I found her on the floor, sobbing loudly.

Truth

I finally opened my eyes to found myself in a hospital room, sitting with Kat and Mia. Mia looked weaker than I had ever seen her and I could feel a burning sensation rushing through my veins. I noticed that Mia was sitting in a chair with a strange IV set up next to her. "I don't even understand why I am putting myself through chemo," Mia mumbled.

Kat looked up from her magazine and then closed it, placing it to the side. "We've talked about this Mimi. The doctor said that you still have a chance. Don't give up so quickly. And keep a positive attitude. Remember?"

"Cancer sucks," Mia practically spat out.

"Well obviously," Kat sighed and held Mia's hand. "If it didn't suck then why would they be looking for a cure?"

Tears filled Mia's eyes and she shrugged. "Guess you're right Kitty Kat," she muttered and then her eyes went wide and she clasped a hand over her mouth.

Kat quickly leaned backwards and retrieved a bedpan that Mia grabbed and threw up into. When she finally caught her breath, she was even weaker than before. "You think if Lucas were here he'd hold my hand?" Mia whispered and Kat sighed heavily.

"Why haven't you called him?" she asked. "Why hasn't he called you? I still don't understand why the two of you broke up."

"Because he deserves better than a girl who is going to die," Mia said under her breath and Kat glared. "I'm sick," Mia went on. "I don't know what's going to happen but I know that Lucas shouldn't have to be sad and wait around for me to either get better or die when he can find a perfectly healthy girl to make him perfectly happy."

"Would you stop speaking like that?" Kat sighed. "Does he even know you're sick?"

Mia looked down at her hands. "He thinks I had a virus," she mumbled. "I told him that I didn't love him and that I was moving so we might as well start fresh."

"You forgot to mention that you have leukemia and you came to New York to get proper treatment by Mom's old Oncologist who I trust," Kat practically hissed and Mia closed her eyes.

The burning feeling started to dull. I sunk down in a seat next to Kat and watched as a nurse pulled back the curtain to tell Mia that she was finished with treatment for the day. She helped Mia undo the fancy wires and then helped her into a wheelchair so Kat could wheel her back to her room. Mia scratched her head and frowned when a few pieces of hair were left in her hand.

"I miss him," she finally admitted.

"I know you do," Kat sighed. "Maybe you should call him."

They rounded the corner to find an elevator and they climbed in. Mia shut her eyes and fell asleep right in the wheelchair. Kat inhaled deeply and there were tears in her eyes.

I stepped onto the elevator and found that Thyme was waiting on the other side. "So how do you feel now?" she asked.

"Like I can never just be happy," I whispered. "Reliving all of my mistakes and regrets is really not as much fun as you would expect," I said sarcastically.

"I know," Thyme agreed. "Trust me, I've seen worse lives than yours."

"Like what?"

"Well there was mine of course. But obviously you probably want to know about a life of this man I helped. He only had one leg and his wife left him because she wanted a man who had two."

"She's an idiot," I muttered.

"Aren't we all?" Thyme sighed and looked over at Mia. "We've both made mistakes in our lives. Guess you're just going to have to see how it works out for you."

"Please don't tell me I'm going to be depressed all over again for the rest of my short freaking life!" I wailed.

Thyme grabbed me and pulled me into a hug before I could say another word. "I know it's difficult," she whispered.

For a split second, I heard a heartbeat. I saw a girl with long, beautiful blond hair, running towards a boy who waited for her. He opened his arms and she threw herself into them. The scent of spices filled my senses and I quickly pulled back. "What was that?" I asked, alarmed.

"It's what I lost," Thyme shrugged. "Maybe your lives sucked. But your afterlife doesn't have to."

I stared at her for a long time and I thought of that woman in her memory. "Neither does yours," I responded. "Your lives don't have to end there either. You can move on."

"This is not about me. It's about you Jane Doe."

Orion

As I blinked, my head actually spun again and I knew that a lot of time must have passed. I was standing in a hospital room again. There was a woman lying in the bed. She looked incredibly weak. She had a bandana on her head and her skin was pale and dry looking. She was so skinny that I didn't know how she even held herself up. Under the bandana, I could tell that she didn't have any hair, and her eyebrows were gone as well.

"Mia?" I gasped and tears pricked my eyes. "Look at me! I look horrible!"

"That's not you anymore," Thyme assured me, and took a seat, watching quietly.

Mia slowly opened her eyes and pushed herself up on her elbows, weakly looking around the room. Kat entered, holding a tray of hospital food that made my stomach turn. I could feel Mia's weakness reverberating through me.

"Hey Mimi," Kat greeted. "I got you some soup and Jell-O."

"Thanks," Mia sighed. "But I'm not hungry."

Her eyes were half-shut and she looked outside, staring into the night. "It's beautiful," Kat murmured, referring to the sky.

"Always is," Mia agreed. "Hey, Kitty-Kat, look at this."

Kat sat on the side of Mia's bed and I did as well. Mia pointed out the window and I looked up at the wonderful stars, slightly hidden by the lights that were on in the room. Kat turned out the light and lay down across the bed, upside down and opposite from Mia. "You see that star over there?"

"Which one?" Kat chuckled.

Mia weakly lifted her arm and pointed at a group of three stars. She explained how the three stars were a belt line. She pointed out the torso and the arms and the sword and shield that the stars seemed to be holding. "That constellation," she breathed. "Is called Orion. He's a hunter. Out of all the constellations that Lucas showed me, Orion is my favorite. There's this whole crazy story of how he was the greatest hunter in the land and he fell in love and was killed by a scorpion or something. It's all Greek mythology, but it always fascinated me. Lucas was so smart. He pretty much knew every single constellation."

Kat nodded slowly and picked at a hangnail. "Do you ever miss him?" she whispered and then quickly continued. "I'm sorry. I didn't mean to bring up a sore topic-"

"That's okay," Mia stopped her, sleepily. "I brought it up. And yes. I miss him all the time. It's been a year and he's still all I think about."

"As I would expect," Kat agreed.

Silence took over the room and I lay down where Mia was in the bed. Of course, I went right through her, but I felt slightly connected to her. As I shut my eyes, I pretended to be a part of her again. "Kitty?" Mia breathed.

"Yeah?" Kat whispered, wiggling her toes near Mia's head.

"I want to go home."

Bargain

"Alright," a nurse said and I found myself in Mia's hospital room. Again.

The nurse was unplugging some wires that were attached to Mia's arm. Kat was filling out a piece of paper. I looked over her shoulder and smiled as I realized that she was signing papers to discharge Mia from the hospital.

"I'm finally going home," Mia whispered dreamily.

She still wore the scarf on her head, but I noticed that her eyebrows were beginning to grow back. She was dying, yet had gained some life back that the chemo stole from her.

"If you need anything, bring her in immediately," a doctor was telling Kat as he collected the papers from her.

Kat thanked him and smiled as she took the wheelchair that Mia was sitting in and began to push her down the hallway. The world seemed like a blur of happiness as we moved forward. I could feel the gleeful energy rushing off of Mia in waves.

"Ready?" Kat asked and Mia replied with a "Hell yeah!"

"Remember," Kat started as they got into an elevator. "This isn't forever. We'll eventually-"

"Have to come back when I get weaker and I need to be taken care of. This is temporary to allow me to get some freedom for a little while," Mia finished for her and smirked. "I know Kitty-Kat. You've given me the speech many times."

Kat giggled. "Lucy and Stan called this morning. They want to come in to see us."

"Cool," Mia sighed. "You so have to drive me around New York so I can really see some of it."

"You've told me," Kat responded, laughing quietly.

The elevator door opened and Kat rolled Mia to the front entrance of the hospital. She froze when she saw the rain falling down in buckets and Mia tensed up. "I'll um... I'll pull the car up," Kat said. "Wait here Mimi."

Mia nodded slowly. "I won't go anywhere."

Mercy

I felt extremely dizzy the next time I appeared in a hospital room and I frowned, realizing that Mia had eventually come back here. It must have been a few years because I couldn't stop my head from spinning. Thyme was standing next to me. I looked in the hospital bed and I was surprised to find Mia with her long hair back. But it was a mess around her head. Her hair didn't hold the life that it used to and her body was so thin I could practically see the outlines of her bones. "I'll be waiting on the other side," was all Thyme said before she disappears.

"Thyme?" I whispered. "*Thyme!*" I shrieked, suddenly afraid to be alone.

I could barely breathe as my world seemed to collapse on top of me. Somebody walked into the room and I turned quickly, not believing what I saw. "Lucas?" I mumbled.

He was broader and had more muscle. His hair was cut shorter as well. But his face had barely changed a bit. His eyes landed on Mia and he froze, placing a hand softly over his mouth. Mia's eyes fluttered open and they were surrounded by dark circles. She had bruises all over her skin. "Lucas?" she rasped and Lucas just watched her with the saddest gaze.

"Kat, um, called me," he said very slowly, almost as if he was afraid that his very words would break her.

Mia was hooked up to so many wires that I didn't even know what was what anymore. I wondered what would happen if she just unplugged all of those wires and set herself free...

"You said it was a virus." Lucas shook his head slowly.

Mia's tired eyes were sad. "I lied."

"I can see that." Lucas gradually made his way next to the bed and sat down in a chair. "It's been a long time."

"It has," Mia croaked. "How long has it been?"

"Three years."

"Time all seems the same to me now. An hour seems like a decade," Mia rasped.

Lucas nodded. "I never expected to see you again," he admitted.

"Same here," Mia agreed. "Why um... why are you here?"

"Like I said... Kat called me. She said you uh... that you weren't doing well and that I should come see you. I was really confused until she told me that you lied to me. I've been wondering for years why you would just break up with me after two years... and now it all makes sense."

"It does?" Mia had tears in her eyes. Lucas nodded. "Lucas I'm so sorry for hurting you. I just didn't want you to have to go through this with me."

"You didn't give me quite enough credit," Lucas sighed. "I um... I was wondering... how much of what you said that day was a lie?"

Mia looked up through heavy eyes that were half-shut. "Every word," she whispered and her eyes were already closing.

Lucas nodded and his phone rang. He pulled it out and glanced at it before shutting it off and slipping it back into his pocket. "Who was that?" Mia questioned.

Lucas coughed and looked at his feet. "That was um... that was my fiancé."

Mia frowned and the tears in her eyes built up more. "Oh," she croaked. "Of course it was."

"Mia, you broke up with me," Lucas reminded her. "Three years ago."

Mia wiped away a tear. "I know," she forced out and her hand shook as she lowered it back to her side. "I just missed you a lot over the years. And now you are here in front of me... and I'm about to lose you all over again."

"Mia," Lucas murmured. "Maybe I shouldn't have come."

"Maybe," Mia agreed but she didn't seem to really believe it. "Maybe you should go home to your fiancé."

Lucas stared for a long moment. "Is that really what you want?" he asked. Mia didn't respond for a long time.

"Does it matter what I want?" she finally asked in response. "I don't really get a say in your life anymore."

Lucas's eyes darkened. "You could have if you would have told me the truth."

"It wouldn't be the same. You'd be miserable."

"I'd be with you. You could be the one I'm about to marry right now!"

"You wouldn't be marrying me. You'd be watching me die!"

"It didn't have to be this way Mia! You chose this!" he snapped and Mia's lips trembled. "I'm sorry I didn't-"

"Maybe you should go," Mia squeaked and her breathing grew heavier. Her heart-monitor accelerated slightly.

"Mia-"

"Lucas, seriously, just go!" she gasped out. It would have been a shout if she had the energy.

Lucas stared at her for a long moment and then sighed. "Mi," he said, tears in his eyes. "I'm sorry we couldn't make it work. Maybe in the next life."

He leaned down and kissed her on the head and then stood to leave the room. "Lucas!" Mia called and he turned for a moment to look at her.

She didn't say anything and they just watched each other for a long time. Lucas finally looked away. "Goodbye Mia," he sighed and left.

"Mercy," Mia shouted and when Lucas didn't return, she broke down into sobs and I felt weak and heartbroken, just watching the scene.

Mia slowly leaned over and ripped out her IV, disconnecting her heart-monitor and all the other wires that connected her to machines. As her weak fingers moved as fast as they could, I began to feel the sensation of her movements. I was fading.

Mia forced herself out of bed and the pain was nearly unbearable. She was moving now, holding onto the wall for support and I followed after her, feeling the wall against my own hands. My feet ached as they moved and my knees shook. My head spun and my stomach heaved, and yet I still kept moving.

Part of me continued to pull away, but as I looked at Mia and her last few minutes on Earth, I couldn't help but want to relive them for just a little bit longer. As Mia rounded the corner to the elevator, and pressed the button to climb on, I shut my eyes, feeling every movement at full force. My bones felt like they might just break under the pressure and I groaned in pain. When I opened my eyes, Mia was climbing off the elevator, pushing her tired body through the main entrance of the hospital and onward to the front door. The censors forced them open at the movement of her body, and the last of me faded away and for a moment, I was connected to Mia again.

I could see Lucas. He was moving farther away, walking through the parking lot towards his car. My knees were shaking hard and I froze in the doorway of the hospital. It was pouring outside and I felt my heart skip a beat. If the rain touched me… then what? I was about to let him get away. He was already blurring into the dark night and I was so far gone already. I moved one foot outside and the rain splashed and hit my skin and I gasped. The water was cold and well… that was pretty much it. It was like taking a cold shower. The rain rinsed off of my skin. It didn't hurt me at all.

It was completely safe.

I forced myself out into the rain, and I cringed but I kept moving. Lucas was now just a dot in the distance, about to climb into his car. "M... m-m-m..." I couldn't get the word out. I was too weak and the rain was too loud and my voice was hidden under its sound.

I took a huge, deep breath, painfully filling my lungs, feeling my abdomen inflate, and as I let the breath out, I let it out in a scream and I shouted, "*Meeeeeerrrrrcccccy!*"

As the scream died off, I found myself feeling weak in the legs and I doubled over, falling forwards to my knees. Lucas's blurry figure continued to move and I felt regret and pain wash over my every sense. But then I realized he was not running away from me.

He was running towards me.

I held on for as long as I could. *He was coming back for me!* I whispered "Mercy" again, breathing weakly.

Lucas was getting closer. The rain water was soaking through my thin sweatshirt and sweatpants. *"Mia?"* I heard his voice from far away.

I began to fall forwards and his arms caught me before I could hit the ground. *"Oh my... Mia what are you doing out here?"*

"Mercy," I whispered.

Did he hear me?

I couldn't feel my hands or my feet. Numbness was spreading through me, moving through my every last nerve and the only thing I could feel was the warm sensation of his hands against my back.

"Help! Somebody help!" Lucas was shouting, holding me close.

"Mercy," I got out.

I could feel myself going. Something was pulling me away, and yet I felt more alive than I had in a long time. My head was resting against Lucas's chest. I didn't know this from feeling it. I knew because I could hear the faint sound of his heartbeat, pulsing quickly.

"Oh no. Stay with me Mia."

"Mercy."

Lucas's face blurred and held itself in my memory. I thought of him and only him and every last bit of me was giving into his hold that was on me.

"Stay with me!"

"Mercy."

"Somebody help me! Please help me!"

"Mer-cy."

"Mia please don't leave me."

"Mer...cy."

"Mia please... I love you!"

And I was gone.

After Life
The Choice

I jolted upwards, my eyes shooting straight open as I screamed, "Mercy!"

I was met with silence that seemed to wrap around me. It was bright, and calm, and strikingly eerie, as if all the sound had been sucked up into a black hole and it took everything else with it... except me.

My eyes slowly roamed around the white nothingness and after a long moment, I sighed with relief. The first time I saw it, it had been terrifying. Now it was comforting. I wanted to stay here, to hold on for a long time in this quiet peacefulness. This must have been a heaven of some sort.

The weakness that was in my bones only moments ago was gone. I felt kind of amazing. No more suffering. No more pain. No more weakness. No more anything. And I couldn't help but feel grateful for it.

I looked around slowly, sighing and staring down at my iridescent, transparent fingers. I wiggled them and felt a breeze rush through them. I knew that I didn't belong here, but I just wanted to stay here forever. Maybe I could just sleep for the rest of eternity in this little bit of peacefulness. I held onto it for as long as I could. Thyme didn't interrupt me. The longing for a heartbeat no longer haunted me. All I needed was this- this timeless, ageless world that held me in its arms and told me that I was going to be okay.

I knew that soon enough I would have to leave here and I felt a little threatened and scared by that thought. I was safe now. I didn't want to leave.

Please just let me be!

I felt the slightest bit of fear inside of me and I realized that I was scared of what came next. I had been through so much. But that was just the difficult part... right? If I just let go now and let my worries go away, I'd be able to make the choice that I needed to make.

My mind suddenly spun as every single last memory of my lives fell into place, like a puzzle of truth and stories. I fell to the ground and held my head as voices and memories rushed forth. I could hear Alex screaming for Devin to stay with her and Lucas screaming for Mia. I could hear Anita's soft voice blending with Pamela's and singing me to sleep. Melanie's peppy voice mixed with Emily's and Kat's. And then I could hear my own thoughts. Alex and Mia and Olivia were all one person, all me.

Patrick isn't so bad- I don't like Devin! I can't- He can read the stars- I hate her- I love him- I can't believe this- Devin please don't leave me- I want to hate him but I can't- I can't tell him the truth...

I grasped my head tighter as the voices faded and I just sat there, listening to the sound of my unnecessary breathing.

"Time to make a choice Jane Doe," Thyme said from behind me.

"What if they didn't choose me?" I asked. "I mean... what are my options?"

I just kept holding my head.

"Jane Doe, they *all* chose you," Thyme explained, kneeling down beside me. "Every one of them. You had a big heart and you let them all in."

My un-beating heart suddenly leaped and I gasped, throwing my hands over my chest. It still didn't beat, but for the first time since it stopped, it strangely felt alive again.

"I can't choose," I got out, lying down against the ground. "How can I?"

"You have to Jane Doe."

I thought of Patrick and my love for him surged. Those beautiful big blue eyes that only held love for me. I wanted to take him into my arms and never let him go. Yes he hurt me, but he never meant it. It was a mental issue. Now we could live together in the afterlife and be happily ever after. I met him in a coat-closet and I'd loved him ever since. We were set up to be married and it was meant to be anyway.

But then I thought of Devin. How much I missed him and how much I still did. We never really gave *us* a try. But could we now? If we didn't work out, would we be stuck? It barely mattered because we would be together. I thought of our last kiss, our only kiss, and I wanted that again. I could feel his lips against mine and I pictured him alive and well in front of me. For the first time, I realized I could still have that. I could have him back. My best friend. The love of my life. But was he the love of my afterlife?

I thought of Lucas. He always felt like my soul mate. He made me smile. He made me laugh. I felt empty after I left him. I loved him with every fiber of my being and I nearly lost him. I broke his heart and he still came back for me. He held me while I took my last breath and never let me go. While I couldn't live without him, he couldn't live without me either. Feeling loved like that was all I ever wanted in life. And was that enough to need an afterlife with him as well?

All of my choices were splayed out in front of me. All of my hopes and dreams and wishes were spinning and calling for me to reach out and grasp a life. And for the first time, I realized that it wasn't only about the love of my life. The others in my life mattered as well. I thought of what, of *whom*, I needed in my afterlife.

"Where will you go after this?" I asked, trying to avoid the choice.

"I'll continue what I've been doing."

"You and I both know that's not what you want," I whispered. "Just try. Please. Promise me you'll at least attempt to try one more time. You don't have to be Taylor anymore. Be happy. Make it better."

"Start a new life," Thyme said.

I couldn't help but smile, but Thyme continued to push for me to choose and it made me sick.

"I can't," I stammered.

"Jane Doe, if you choose... I'll consider trying again, okay?"

As happy as that made me, I still didn't feel right about all of this.

"I can't just choose one of them Thyme."

Thyme stared at me and then smiled in understanding. She wrapped her arms around me and held me for a long time. I could smell the herbs on her from her last life slowly fading away. "You already have," she whispered and disappeared.

My eyes went wide. "Thyme? Thyme!"

I spun around and around, trying to find her, and suddenly I heard footsteps behind me.

Epilogue

"Alex?" a voice said softly.

My entire body stiffened. A chill ran down my spine and my heart leaped into my throat.

"Devin," I whispered.

I slowly turned to find him standing in front of me.

My hand trembled as I extended it and touched the side of his cheek. He felt so real.

"You died," I said and my throat constricted.

"So did you," Devin responded. "Three times."

The emptiness around me took on colors of pink, blue, purple, orange, and red. It was a sunset. I quickly wrapped my arms around Devin's torso and held on tightly. He gripped me to him and I buried my face into his shoulder and let out a soft cry.

He smelled like Devin.

I felt him pulling away, and I was about to protest, but then he was kissing me. I felt all the time spent without him drifting away. He was here, and I was here, and we were together.

He pulled away only to whisper, "I love you too."

I swallowed thickly. "I missed you," I said through my tears.

Devin took my hand and pulled me along and I held onto him tightly as I followed him into the open, beautiful vastness of Mercy's sunset.

Mercy's Sunset